Photograph by Bjorn Schild

About the author

Stephen James Boyd is a writer and artist, born and raised in Edinburgh, Scotland. Having travelled extensively for over three decades he has now settled in Spain after being adopted by his black cat Frankie.
Chasing Faith is his first book.

CHASING FAITH

Stephen James Boyd

CHASING FAITH

Vanguard Press

VANGUARD PAPERBACK

© Copyright 2023
Stephen James Boyd

The right of Stephen James Boyd to be identified as author of
this work has been asserted by him in accordance with the
Copyright, Designs and Patents Act 1988.

All Rights Reserved

No reproduction, copy or transmission of this publication
may be made without written permission.
No paragraph of this publication may be reproduced,
copied or transmitted save with the written permission of the
publisher, or in accordance with the provisions
of the Copyright Act 1956 (as amended).

Any person who commits any unauthorised act in relation to
this publication may be liable to criminal
prosecution and civil claims for damages.

A CIP catalogue record for this title is
available from the British Library.

ISBN 978 1 80016 832 9

Vanguard Press is an imprint of
Pegasus Elliot Mackenzie Publishers Ltd.
www.pegasuspublishers.com

This is a work of fiction. Names, characters, businesses, places, events and
incidents are either the products of the author's imagination or used in a
fictitious manner. Any resemblance to actual persons, living or dead, or
actual events is purely coincidental.

First Published in 2023

Vanguard Press
Sheraton House Castle Park
Cambridge England

Printed & Bound in Great Britain

Dedication

To my daughter Sara for her incessant stream of inspiration.

Acknowledgements

To the teachers who give confidence wrapped up in experiential knowledge.

Introduction

Asteroid 52 QG hurtled through space at twenty-nine thousand and five-hundred kilometers per hour, the blackness opening up before it like a wall-less tunnel welcoming traffic. The collision had no pre-emption; no hazard warning lights blinked in futility.

Three thousand and forty kilometers above Earth, Asteroid 52 QG smashed into the orbiting satellite, a gift of destiny from the Universe presented raw, devoid of ribbons and bows.

The diminutive spy satellite placed in Earth's orbit twenty-seven years previously, under the pretence of China's own Web Net design, had performed its functions well, flawlessly circling the planet transmitting data to Chinese generals in need of every advantage possible in their quest for a hold on global power.

The force of the impact from the asteroid had burst the satellite's gas thruster tank, designed to minutely but significantly keep this spy technology on its intended orbital trajectory. The sudden impact and the subsequent propulsion gas release from the tank had jettisoned the satellite onto a new and dangerous path.

Onboard computer systems had fizzled briefly in their protective casings and monitors back on Earth had turned black all at once.

Travelling at twenty-eight thousand kilometers per hour, this new trajectory was eating up the black vacuum of space, the technicians now only guessing at the arc and speed of the now out-of-control, 1.75-ton mass.

Panic had enveloped the entire control room. Raging red faces shouted at the back of heads, many held in upturned palms, trying to hide in disbelief at the stark truth of the event.

They had lost control. Heads would roll but these were just the consequences on the ground. The potential for catastrophe had been propelled into occupied space and nobody knew where the ripples of this collision would wreak their havoc.

Chapter 1

The state of the world was a sorry one. Society had collapsed, civilisation was no longer civil; fear and necessity were the new commanders. With global plagues spurring ever-increasing death tolls, wars between countries battling for dominant power only extrapolated the body count.

Industry and finance, as they were known at the turn of the century, were no longer operating; cash had disappeared, shoved aside in the early 2020s by touchless technologies. Born from this cashless society were the credits systems, ravaged from their inception by the greedy fingers of corruption. The speed at which human life on Earth had collapsed was astonishing but the rise of AI technologies and the move towards other planetary colonisation was even more astounding in its rapidity. Bionic humanoids now far outnumbered flesh-and-blood humans and AI bots outnumbered both combined.

Global-power restructuring was the norm, Russia and China uniting and tearing apart. The United States had lost all hope of unity, its citizens scattered, many dying in underground bunkers of their own rushed design. Off-grid communities, armed to the teeth, often bit themselves into extinction. Oppression reigned; rebel factions that formed were cut down and reformed. Global warming was crisping the surface of the planet with unpredicted efficacy. Increased solar activity had rendered the electronics of old inadequate and communications succumbed to a decade of constant revival from the dead. Murder and suicide rates, especially of the elderly, were pushed to the brink by the chaos, leaving only the strongest and most blood thirsty.

Life on Earth had truly become survival of the fittest.

Oil and gas-rich countries had little worth: they were swallowed whole and spat out by a succession of dominators. Hospitals existed only for bionic humanoid procedures; mainly soldiers of the governing military bodies battling for the last footholds of control. The grey areas of government spending were whitewashed into oblivion, with debt as inevitable as the death of the planet. Latent technology had been released when the wars had increased, not only to enhance military capabilities but with a vision to extricate survivors before there was no-one left to extricate. All resources targeted planetary evacuation.

AI bots had first begun construction on Mars in 2032. Known as the Progeny Mission, five space stations circled in calculated orbits, spun out like Saturn's rings, designed as jump points to the new colonies. Global schooling was mandatory and oriented specifically to cosmology and all subjects relating to human survival in space. Religion, having been outlawed, had gone underground, feeding faith to the hopeless.

The Reverend Gerard Sinclair, an ambitious, self-proclaimed minister, was the leading light of hope for his small congregation and he operated in a somewhat tolerated grey area between out lawlessness and the need for man's belief in the Almighty, a faith propelling humanity towards salvation.

Dr Gerard Sinclair, as he was officially titled, was a geomagnetic scientist of the highest order; hence his placement on the Progeny Mission. 'Reverend' Sinclair was the address that he demanded of the few followers in his congregation.

Standing tall at six feet and seven inches, too tall in fact for his skinny frame, gave him a physical ratio similar to a broomstick with a watermelon impaled on the end of it. However, it was not his height that dominated his congregation but his passionate orations of God's plan and how he had been chosen by the Almighty to save and guide humanity from its own destruction.

Staring out from sunken sockets, his own windows to the soul were steely grey and full of intent, his out-of-control, mousy-brown hair sprouted from a large, bone-plated skull at opposing angles, as if trying to avoid contact with its neighbour. Beneath these bony plates lay Sinclair's ego, wanting only to grasp control and leadership of a humanity soon to be unique to planet Mars and the habitable Brown Dwarfs found in the neighbouring solar system, a mere ten light-years away. His ego controlled his manipulations of his followers and disciples, as he liked to think of them. Men and women of science are not easily attuned to the words of God but the atrocities and the devastation of change over the last few decades, inflicted upon the planet and its inhabitants, had raised the bar of hope high enough that some clung or latched onto the shirt tails of faith.

With his deep, compelling voice and intellectual reasoning, Reverend Sinclair succeeded in gathering some lambs into his flock, his prized and most ardent disciple being his wife Deborah. Twelve years his junior, at thirty-seven, she was his most sacrificial of lambs.

After graduating university from Missouri University of Science and Technology, in Rolla, Sinclair began preaching his ideals and beliefs. In 2027, at the dynamic age of twenty-four years old, he landed a contract with the Midwest television station, MWBC, and moulded himself into their prime-time television evangelist. Over the next three years, he reaped a large number of followers and also the benefits of a small fortune, enabling him to brush shoulders with the rich and famous. Attending one particular convention, set up out of compassion for the world's millions of orphans, Sinclair had met the entrepreneurial trillionaire and head of Branson Enterprises, Howard Branson. During this short encounter, Branson had told the Reverend of his investments in space and alluded to the cosmos being the next Wild-West Frontier. They had laughed and joked about the possibility of Sinclair becoming a king on his own planet. This jovial exchange had only served to tease and fuel Sinclair's insatiable ego and render him a slave to its greed. The idea of ultimate power had been sown and he was determined to reap the harvest.

However, shortly after this brief encounter, in the summer of 2030, Sinclair was the target of a media persecution over a reported sexual assault upon a male member of his congregation. The subsequent scandal lasted several months and although never brought before a judge – an out-of-court settlement had been reached – the scandal was enough for MWBC TV to drop Sinclair from its listings.

It was not the money that Sinclair missed but the control and the power over his believers. He had truly felt like a king serving God. He needed to figure out how to get into space, nearer to God and nearer to his planetary kingdom.

With government announcements stating an upcoming law prohibiting religious practices for the benefit of global security, religion was retreating underground. Sinclair retreated along with it and with the purpose of educating himself on the space program, he set about spreading the joys of faith to his die-hard followers from the shadows. The need for infiltration and for secrecy grew, his darkness only deepening; the only brightness, his sharp focus.

Steadily, over the next few years, Sinclair upgraded his own education and that of his disciples. Handpicked for their intellectual potential and in the case of some of the female members of his flock, their breeding potential, Sinclair nurtured his cell of willing progenitors.

The Global Confederation, in 2035, implemented mandatory schooling of the cosmic sciences with the view to training as many minds as possible to enable a successful planetary evacuation and fruitful relocation. Sinclair enrolled his students in various facilities with the outcome that by 2051, he and thirty-five of his disciples had been enrolled into the space programme and were destined for the newly constructed colonies on Mars.

October 2052 was when Dr Gerard Sinclair and his lovely wife found themselves on board Space Station 2, having transferred from Space Station 1 nine months previously. They were now starting the next nine-month transitional period before jumping another forty-four million miles at a time, closer to Mars through Space Stations 3, 4 and 5, sequentially.

Having lost three members (two drop outs and a death) and a further six who had remained on Space Station 1, Sinclair was hard at work trying to glean more followers from the three hundred and fifty human personnel on board. This work was frustrating and was bearing little fruit. AI bots monitored all areas of the station and many scientists on their way to the colonies considered themselves to be in little need of saving.

Down to twenty-six members, including his wife Deborah, this was still going to be sufficient for his plans. Two members of his tribe were pregnant; one in her last trimester and showing visible signs of discomfort, her taut belly skin squeezed into her flight suit, had shown the first signs of new life by experiencing kicking against the walls of her womb some three months earlier. She was going to give birth to a space baby.

An optimistic air pervaded the whole space station. An ease of social interactions, steady study for the future to come, and daily duties and preparations filled most of the time with an underlying feeling of united purpose. It did feel like everyone had a purpose, a role to play in the colonisation of a new planet. The possibilities bound everyone on board with an embracing unity. The only anxiety lay with the still-bizarre interactions with the AI bots, their presence felt everywhere. Their proven intellectual capabilities were enormous and left even the smartest and sharpest on board feeling dumb: this distilled into wariness.

The space station housed three hundred and fifty humans in transition, eighty bionic humanoids, comprising mostly teachers, technicians and pilots, and a further one hundred and seventy AI bots maintaining the space station's orbital operations, communication links, security, medical and food facilities. Unlike the International Space Station from the turn of the century, which was manned by six human personnel and shaped in an 'H' configuration, these new space stations, although all differing in complexity and function, were basically constructed in the shape of a motorcycle wheel, with a central hub housing the control centre and medical facilities. Joined to an outer ring by corridors, each spoke with its own specific purpose. The outer ring consisted of launching and landing bays, and dorms for the human population, and was dotted with observation platforms for use by the astronomer lecturers, as well as passenger pleasure. Spinning like frisbees through space at twenty-five thousand kilometers per hour, they resembled the London Eye lying on its side, although their diameters differed by about two kilometers and the weight disparity was about 7.6 million kilograms.

Humanoid lecturers with data uplinks on specific science subjects taught daily compulsory lessons to classrooms filled with 'pure' humans. Their digital and physical enhancements were disgusting to some and the envy of others. Many of the bionic humanoids had military backgrounds and often their brain chips were the result of injuries sustained from the conflicts raging on the Earth's surface below, but more often than not chips were prescribed, without consent, to gain an advantage over the enemy. The AI bots, however, had changed everything; they were geared and built for specific operations, the variances decided by the learning protocols introduced into the bots' written code. War Bots had turned many battlefield tables and the battles see-sawed as clashes between machines that thought like chess masters struggled to find the best strategy, the results ending often in super-destructive stalemates.

Medic Bots were of incredible value to the humans, dispatching nanobots into the biological systems to perform non-invasive surgeries and wiping out the ever-modifying plague viruses of the 20s.

One of the more surreal sights on the Space Station was witnessing an AI bot charging. Most bots had servo-motion charging but sometimes this was not sufficient to fully compensate the energies dispelled and the sight of a bot charging from a digit port had an oddity about it. Standing in standby mode with its finger inserted into the wall port always appeared bizarre, like pressing the button on an old elevator and simultaneously being frozen in time.

Life on the stations was luxurious; the food was of a high nutritional value, some fresh from the farm labs on board and every need was catered for. Bodies were lean and well exercised. The many restrictions – for example, the prohibition of Earth-bound communications, compulsory duties and activities – were all complimented into disregard by the many freedoms on board and from the prospect of a future born from a devastating and disastrous past.

All on board were only too aware that it was up to them to make the difference and the success of the new colonies was at the forefront of every mind; minds of grey matter and neural pathways but also minds of circuitry.

Chapter 2

Had it carried on along its projected path, Asteroid 52QG would have broken up in the Earth's atmosphere and spattered the Indian Ocean with its celestial pebbles, like skipping stones on the surface of a forest pond. Nothing so tranquil was to be its fate. Gravitational distortion had bent its path, sweeping its trajectory at a forty-two-degree curvature and sending it headlong into the Chinese satellite, where it fractured upon impact into three smaller blocks, creating detritus from the size of a basketball to dust particles. This explosion of rock and ice carried onward, now pushing the mangled remains of the satellite ahead of it, like a tugboat manoeuvring a cargo ship to dock. Immediately ahead and closing at speed from the opposite direction was Space Station 2.

The impact was sudden and violent.

Professor Steed stood at the lectern, his left hand curling round the slope that held his notes, his right hand, a bionic prosthesis up to the elbow, gesticulating like an Italian at a Sunday family gathering, gesturing his words to the class.

A series of thuds echoed from the corridor, the vibrations of the outer ring giving the air the bass resonance of a rock concert, lasting only moments before a chorus of ripping, screeching and explosive percussion tore through the doors. Alarm sirens blasted at steady intervals, lights flashing behind air-lock doors.

Steed's prosthesis gripped the sloping edge of the desktop leaving small dents as a testament to his will to remain upright while all else around him cartwheeled. Finding his voice again, he yelled for everyone to make their way to the exit. The doors, buckled in their frames, allowed only a single person to squeeze through. Looking to his right as he popped his head through the gap, Steed faced sealed doors; airlocks that had automatically sealed off the passageway after the breach in the hull had occurred. A midnight-black triangle of outer space stared back at him through the airlock window.

"Let's go!" he urged, looking over his shoulder, "Left, to the jump bays – these airlock doors are sealed."

With this, Steed slipped through the gap and ventured down the hallway, looking back to see that the rest of the class was following. Up ahead similar classrooms were emptying. More noise erupted behind him as he was lifted into the air, staring down the tubular chute that was the hallway as the outer ring tore free from two of the spoked corridors connecting them to the central hub. An airlock slammed shut behind him, his body bouncing off what, moments before, had been the ceiling. Bursts of air escaped in billows from his lungs with the force of the impacts. A further jolt flung his flailing torso, spread-eagled, onto an observation window, where he clung like a spider with no obvious barrier between himself and the inhospitable universe. Like a starfish clinging to the reef in a strong tidal current, he held his position long enough to witness the twisted wreckage of the space station. A gigantic bite had been taken from this huge space doughnut.

Bodies and fragments of the outer ring floated beneath him like balloons released at a fair.

"Sean!" His name rang in his own ear for a moment before he could tear his gaze from the carnage.

"Sean!" she shouted again, her hand held out as if begging for food scraps.

Deb Sinclair was standing in front of him on the wall of the corridor. Her long, copper-red hair, normally held in a tight bun, was cascading down the side of her elfin face, her sky-blue eyes flecked with amber, as if a sudden breeze had blown some freckles from the bridge of her nose, allowing them to settle and sink into the aquamarine pools of her irises. Urging him to her with her stare, Steed grasped reality and her outstretched hand. Debs' lips, full and coated in a scarlet red matt lipstick, reminiscent of the Rockabilly Era of the last century, formed round the words rushing from her mouth.

"We need to hurry: we need to go now. The space station is tearing itself apart," she panted, tugging at his arm. As he rose, Steed glimpsed one of his students who, only minutes before, had been attentively listening to his lecture but whose body was now gliding into the forever of space on the other side of the window.

Jogging along beside Debs towards the flight bays, Steed asked, "What happened?"

"I have no idea," she replied, "but we have to get the hell out of here and now." Up ahead, Dr Sinclair was ushering people into Jump Bay 12.

"Come on!" he bellowed at them. They ran past him through the airlock and into the Space Plane. Two more passed Sinclair, panicked looks on their faces.

Finally, the other half of the twin, bionic humanoids appeared in the corridor; Russian brothers who had served in the military and whose cerebral implants allowed them the capacity to fly anything. If it had been built, the twins could fly it.

With the other half of this twin team already on board and preparing for flight, Serge was all Sinclair was waiting for.

"Faster, Serge. Faster!" urged the doctor. With another dozen or more people running to the bay, Sinclair pushed the button to close the doors, picking up the fire extinguisher from the wall mount with the intent of disabling the door. AI Bot 131, a security bot, stood in the doorway. Stabbing with all his might, Sinclair struck a resounding blow to its face, sending it backwards into the corridor wall behind it. The door hissed shut and Sinclair unleashed another powerful blow on the operating pad, effectively rendering the doors forever sealed. Slowly stepping backwards, faces appeared at the doors' windows, screaming in silence, barely audible thuds from their panicked pounding echoing in the still of the airlock around him. Behind the disbelieving heads of the irrelevant, appeared AI Bot 131, its faceplates already unbuckling the contortions and dents left by the base of the fire extinguisher, stopping only with a small crescent moon left under its left eye; almost, it seemed, as a reminder of the blow received from Dr Sinclair. The bot's protocols already changed from the normal protect-and-assist to the mode of pursue and detain. Dr Sinclair and AI Bot 131 exchanged a momentary acknowledgement before Sinclair turned and ran to the end of the airlock, sealed the doors and stepped into the Space Plane.

Striding down the centre of the plane, between the rows of his devotees, struggling against adrenaline to buckle their harnesses, he shouted, "Prepare for immediate departure!" He then accessed the cockpit and said to the twins, "The airlock has malfunctioned. We cannot take any more passengers on board. We have to leave now."

The twins, already linked to the plane's systems, to each other, and Alexi having already shown Serge the digital footage of Sinclair disabling the airlock, simply looked at each other. Both said, simultaneously, "Return to your seat, Dr Sinclair. Take-off is imminent."

The twins were identical: shaven, bald heads; both wore the same brand of aviator sunglasses, covering the same optical implants that enabled night vision, heat signature detection, optical zoom configurations, and even infra reds and violets. The only recognisable distinction between the Silchenko brothers was that Serge had *Matb* – Russian for 'Mother' – tattooed across the back of his left hand and Alexi had *Oteu*, signifying Father, inked across his right hand. If wearing gloves, they were as indistinguishable as they were inseparable.

Their hands spread on top of the palm-plates, their fingertips held by small steel hoops, they were now part of the Space Plane's complex systems; a trine, as one, linked together by thought.

Let's do this, they thought to each other and the ten-to-zero countdown began.

Seated on the left of Professor Steed, Deb Sinclair was struggling with her five-point harness. As the 'ten' of the countdown sounded, she blurted, "Sean, can you help me?" mild panic tainting her plea. Unbuckling and standing over her, Sean Steed untangled the harness, his knuckles brushing across Deb's breasts as he clicked the buckles into place. Both nipples had reacted but oddly her right nipple, now thumping hard and luckily covered by the belt strap, had sensed, it seemed, the touch of his real hand. Flushed, her eyes darted up to meet his, golden brown rings surrounding his dilated pupils.

"Thank you." Her lips blew the words as 'four' sounded from the comms relayers.

With everyone seated and poised, the Space Station gave another lurch as the disintegration accelerated, rocking it on its moorings.

'One.' The outside of Deb's pinky finger sought Sean's, then the feeling was silent. Like an ocean swell beneath a row boat, the space plane disengaged, banking away from the bulk of the station. Deb let her finger cross over Sean's, amazed by the sensation and focus, whilst out of the window, below them now, chaos and destruction reigned. The Space Station looked more like a corkscrew of broken DNA than a motorcycle wheel. The central hub spiked with torn-off corridors drifting in spirals away from them. What had happened? And what were they to do now? Only one man on board was forming an idea in answer to the latter.

Chapter 3

Designed as jump ships between the space stations, the space planes had seating for three hundred passengers and AI Bot crew. Each space station had four space planes making the forty-four million-kilometre trips between stations, the longest leg being the final journey to Mars. Shaped like the Concorde aeroplanes of the last century, they were smooth triangles, like an older cousin might build for you when playing paper aeroplanes. Propelled by the Quantum Jump Mechanics System, the trips could be incredibly fast but problems still occurred with the human passengers and the less-efficient Pulsar systems were used, increasing the journey times considerably but ensuring the safe arrivals of the vital human cargo. The interior of the planes was roomy and purposeful, a practical elegance enhanced by the off-white tones and subtle lighting systems, removing any glare into smoothness; adjustable candlelight at its finest with holographics, widely used for communications and entertainment, the Business and First Class of old, rendered primitive. Each widely spaced chair, equipped with passenger voice recognition, could be adjusted by command into a bed, with covering canopy, gliding from the floor to surround, pod-like, for any passenger requiring privacy or indulging in inflight entertainment, information or rest. The only thing not dispensed directly was drinks. Any fluids requested or required were served by the AI Bot crews.

Three of the four space planes from Space Station 2 and two escape pods had managed to disengage and leave behind the explosive destruction. The fourth space plane had become stranded by its own dock-locking mechanism and all on board were presumed dead. The two pilotless escape pods would automatically set a course for Space Station 1. Communication with the central hub of SS2 had been severed moments after the catastrophic impact from the spy satellite and asteroid debris. Survivor numbers were being tallied, communications between the space stations and the jump planes and pods had been established. Two of the planes were to proceed to Space Station 3, the twins' jump plane was commanded to proceed to Space Station 4, a longer route, passing the Brown Dwarf Beatrice 1, named after the citizen astronomer who had discovered its presence. This decision would allow rescue crews access to greater numbers of survivors.

Serge, relieved that Dr Sinclair had waited for him, pressed his ring finger on the control pad.

The Reverend Sinclair, enclosed in his pod, was wrestling ideas into some semblance of order, deep in his mind. Surprised by the appearance of the floating holographic earbud, he touched it with his fingertip, Serge's voice entering his head.

"Ahh, Dr Sinclair. Good afternoon." Serge's Russian accent drifted between his ears. "Dr Sinclair, I want to thank you for waiting for me, so that I could join my brother at the helm."

Sinclair did not respond immediately, suspicious of the call.

"Of course," he replied, his mind racing.

Serge continued. "Could you please join us in the cockpit: we have some information for you to digest."

Sinclair's paranoia and curiosity piqued. How much did the twins know concerning the moments before departure? He replied in the affirmative.

"I shall come immediately." His holographic bud flickered once and disappeared.

Thoughts streamed through his mind, his ego stroking itself with plans for manipulation. *Maybe I can use these humanoids to my advantage: having pilots of a jump plane on my side could be very useful.* As the pod dome retracted, he rose, his long legs carrying him swiftly towards the front of the plane. Sinclair eyed most of his congregation, a smile privately twitching at his lips. Approaching the cockpit door, it slid sideways, allowing him access, gliding closed behind him with only the faintest of hisses.

Alexi glanced over his shoulder and motioned with his head for the doctor to take a seat, a stool rising from the floor beside him.

"Doctor, we have been asked by Control Hub 4 to plot a course to its space station. We are now on that course. I believe this will buy you a little time."

"Time? Why would–"

Serge swiftly cut in. "Please do not interrupt, Doctor. We know what you have done."

A transparent panel, its border lit with a faint glow, emerged between the pilots. Images appeared on the screen, the cockpit lights dimming to allow a crisp, clean picture. It showed Serge jogging towards the camera, his sunglasses tilting up towards the lens and a momentary smile spreading across his face as he passed beneath. The focus was now on Dr Sinclair at the far end of the airlock, unhooking a fire extinguisher from its wall mount. Sinclair had replayed the next few seconds in his mind several times already. The panel dimmed and Serge spoke up.

"The humans that you left behind, Doctor, are more than likely dead. This will create a large problem for you when we arrive at Space Station 4." Serge let this hang in the atmosphere before continuing. "Rescue teams have been dispatched from SS3 for the fifty-seven humans and the six humanoids that they hope to find alive. We know that will not be the case."

"What do you want?" interrupted Sinclair.

"Let us be frank with you, Doctor. We lack for nothing, but we share your – shall we say – dislike for the AI Bots. And you will be interested to know that AI Bot 131 and six others in its team have plotted a course in line with our own. It seems your new acquaintance wants to talk with you in private and alone." A chill crept through Sinclair's spine, like ice crystals forming on a flagpole.

"Alexi can easily erase the data feed, and will – just to show our gratitude for being reunited. AI 131 and his ship are following you, with SS4's permission under the guise that they are to protect and assist, but Alexi and I can read that this is not the mode under which they are operating. You, Doctor, are being hunted".

The stark reactions to his actions sinking deep into his stomach, waves of nausea swept over Sinclair, paling his gaunt face and adding a sticky perspiration that crept over his scalp.

"Go now, Doctor. Attend to your people. My debt to you is now paid but your problems are only just beginning." With this the twins swivelled, facing forward as the door behind Sinclair swished open. Relieved and burdened at the same time, the brothers had bought him some time. He must use it wisely.

An announcement of their projected flight plan sounded in each booth as Sinclair surveyed and attended to his flock.

Sarah reached for Sinclair's arm, tears streaming down her cheeks, snot streaked across her face. "Tony, he didn't make it. . ." she howled.

Kneeling beside her, the Reverend Sinclair gripped her trembling shoulders and offered commiserations.

"Sweet child, Tony has gone before us to pave the way to our future. He will never be forgotten." Kissing her forehead, he stood. "You must rest, we have God's work to do." As she slumped back into her chair, he extricated himself and checked on Tasha, her swollen belly free of the harness and tilted back fruitlessly in search of comfort.

"How is Daniel Junior?" he enquired of Tasha and Daniel.

"Eager to get out, Reverend, but safer inside, I think," answered Tasha. "What happened?" she asked, gripping Daniel Senior's hand a little tighter.

"The stepping stones to our future have taken another path, my dear. Your faith will help guide us. Be strong," Sinclair announced, feeling his confidence rise, if only from the sound of his own protestations.

Eyeing the back of his wife's red hair, leaning over Professor Steed, he marched towards them. Steed had his head tilted back while Deborah leant over him, cleaning a gash on Sean's head, above his left eye.

"Glad you could join us, Professor," Sinclair forced the words through a grimace. "I am sure my wife will administer to your needs; she is a fine care-giver," he continued, catching Deborah's eye and nodding his encouragement. Sinclair needed to think and strode away to his chair pod, not seeing the blush that had risen on his wife's neck. His mind, riddled with the memory of AI Bot 131's threatening stare, its mode having switched to pursuit.

Professor Sean Steed was a widower. His wife of just three short years was killed in a boating accident on Lake Bolsena whilst holidaying in Italy. In the ensuing panic and in his attempt to rescue his wife, Sean had lost his right arm below the elbow to a speedboat propeller. Devastated with grief, he had left Massachusetts, where he had met and courted his wife while attending Harvard and returned to his home city of Wilmington, a watery jewel in Delaware.

Over the next few years, the twenty-five-year-old Steed had recovered fast from his injury but the loss of his wife cut a deeper wound: this showed outwardly as the first signs of greying to his thick black hair. The rehabilitation and fitting of his bionic prosthesis had set Steed adrift into a river of uncertainty. Along with his wife, their plans for the future were lost. For a spell, self-destruction manifested itself, by degree, in bars and bad choices. This did not last for long. Playing an eligible bachelor did not suit his broken heart nor his style. Tattooing the remainder of his right arm to the shoulder, blending his hi-tech prosthesis into a bio-borg creation in ink, allowed Sean to accept his appendage as whole and as his own. With his mind now settled and his body feeling its vitality, he returned to his passion, Marine Biology. At thirty-years old, he still had a lot to offer and his intellect craved learning. The next year, in 2035, Sean Steed was back at Harvard specialising in Planetary Marine Biology, the planetary part being in the new mandatory curriculum. Excelling through focused determination, Professor Sean Steed had found himself, a decade later, on the Progeny Program and had been lecturing for the last seven years aboard Space Station 2.

Perhaps it was the madness of the immediate circumstances or the gentleness of her touch, but Deb Sinclair was healing not only Sean's torn forehead, but a much deeper wound.

Deb Sinclair, however, had scars of her own.

Mrs Sinclair next tended to the pregnant women, both uninjured but clearly shaken, as was everyone. The majority of Reverend Sinclair's band of followers had made it on board with only a few exceptions. Tony, David, and a girl named Christine were missing. Tony they knew for sure was dead; the others presumed so. Twenty-one members plus the Reverend, the twin humanoids and Professor Steed were all alive and fortunate to have reacted so quickly to the disaster. Thoughts turned to the lost and slowly to their own futures on Space Station 4 and beyond.

Deb Sinclair, having handed out water and nutrition pouches to everyone, returned to her chair, easing past the sleeping professor, raised her pod canopy and slowly drifted into an exhausted sleep state.

Deborah Devaroux, as she had been known before her marriage, had a strength, chiselled from her rocky life.

At fourteen years of age, in 2029, in the spring of her adolescence, Deborah had been brutally raped. In the four and a half minutes the savage attack had taken, it had flipped her world upside down and changed her everything, forever. The assault on her body and soul had taken place in the dark shadows of a reading room in a convention centre in Georgia. The only illumination was a single brass reading light with a green glass shade. Her forehead pressed against the desk, her ember red hair warmed by the lamp bulb, she was taken roughly from behind, her attacker, thrusting, tearing her hymen and her innocence, until spent. Not a word spoken. In the few seconds afterwards, her body and mind shaken to the core, she slid from the desk, her blood and his semen oozing from between her pale thighs. As she slumped to the floor, she saw his face, lit by the column of light from the corridor while he checked both ways as if casually crossing a road. It was a face she would never forget.

The following years were splattered with heavy rains that this sudden storm had brought.

Pregnant from the incident, Deborah, her parents and her dignity had ripped apart at the seams. Just fifteen, after a difficult birth that left her womb to be forever barren, her daughter was taken by the State. Deborah, unconscious during the emergency birthing surgery, left the hospital having never seen or held her child. The only connection now between mother and daughter were the microchips inserted by the State to identify the orphan and the donating mother. All other connections were severed, along with the umbilical cord. It was for the best. That is what everybody had kept saying.

The family moved to Houston Texas, like criminals on a witness-protection program, trying to leave the horrors behind; a U-Haul trip away from and to a new life.

Under these new circumstances and surroundings, Deborah responded remarkably well – better than the parents, who were later to divorce, torn apart by shame, blame and anger. Deb, however, completed high school then attended Chambertin University College of Nursing in Houston. Her life was full, albeit devoid of sexual relations, preferring to study over partying with her co-eds. An intensity of purpose, of destiny, burned inside her, feeding her, giving her a noticeable inner strength. She had a purpose and she knew exactly what he looked like.

All was quiet and subdued on the space plane, many of the twenty-three passengers on board fitfully sleeping under their pods.

Gerard Sinclair, however, was wide awake. Sinclair had studied many of the hundreds of Brown Dwarfs, dotted in the shadows of the bigger stars and planets, in the hope of finding one suitable for his own kingdom. Ahead Beatrice 1, although habitable, did not suit his current predicament. He had two major problems and one slim chance at solving them both. Amazed at his own logistical and tactical prowess, he went through the current plan in his head once again.

Problem 1: arriving at SS4, this would see me immediately detained and held accountable for my actions. This cannot happen.

Problem 2: the AI Security Patrol Ship is intent on my detainment and accountability. I have to shake them off.

Solution... Okay, who am I kidding? An act of desperation. Let's call it what it is.

Popping the lid-retract button on his pod, clinging in hope to his powers of persuasion, Dr Sinclair strode in the direction of the only two beings with the power to potentially solve his immediate dilemmas – the twin brothers Silchenko.

Chapter 4

The Silchenko twins were brought up in the countryside on a small farm outside Moscow. Their parents scraped a living from the land. Their father owned one second-hand suit, two sizes too big and their mother alternated her two well-worn dresses one week at a time. The twins helped in all respects and were generally good boys. One cool, late autumn afternoon in October, a government vehicle drove into the farmyard. Two men in dark, government-issued uniforms, banged on the door and asked to speak with Mr Pavel Silchenko. After an hour they left, handing Mr Silchenko a weighty envelope.

"What did they want?" questioned Anika, his wife.

"Come, let us sit down. Call the boys – I have news that concerns all of us." Once they were all seated, the brothers and their mother ogling, with curiosity, the bulky envelope sitting in the centre of the table before them, Pavel Silchenko began.

"Our boys," he started, addressing Anika and letting his eyes fall upon their sons, "have been chosen for special military training." The boys' eyebrows shot skyward and Mrs Silchenko's fingers touched the tip of her nose, covering her gaping mouth. "In two days' time, we will leave this steading forever." Pavel paused, holding his hands out in front of himself to stall any interruptions and questions. "The decision has been made by President Vladimir Putin himself." Pavel leaned forward and placed his hand on top of the envelope. "In this envelope are one hundred thousand rubles; more money than we can ever make in our lifetimes." The boys were now fidgeting and nudging each other with their elbows. A tear had sprung from Mrs Silchenko's eye.

Pavel continued. "We are to move to Moscow to a furnished, two-bedroom apartment." He paused to indicate that the boys should calm down and moved his other hand to rest upon his wife's arm.

"In three months, when our sons turn thirteen, they will leave us for special military training and in all likelihood," he gripped her arm tighter, "we will not be reunited until our deaths." Silence fell upon the room like dusk without a sunset. Anika was the first to speak. She stood, teardrops running freely, dripping from her cheekbones, a smile spread across her face.

"My darling sons – my pride in you both will shine forever. Russia has chosen you, my sweet children, but before I release you to your destinies, let me hug you close to my heart." At this the boys lunged forward, hugging their mother, their tears soaking her apron.

Two days later, they left for the journey to the apartment, a six-storey block on Sadovaya Street. When

Pavel had opened the envelope, there was not only the rubels but a note and a small business card from a tailor's shop, with a voucher, explained in the note, for a tailor-made suit.

The next three months had been a roller-coaster of emotion, sprinkled with some of the most memorable family times, moments only money could buy. Set for life, the two pairs – parents and sons – were about to part ways forever. On the morning of their thirteenth birthday, the same vehicle that had driven into the Silchenko farm yard ninety-three days earlier came to collect the boys and drove them away, waving to their parents through the narrow rear window, towards the military base where, over the next few years, the teenage twins would be moulded mentally and bionically enhanced physically, into two of Russia's finest pilots.

Dr Sinclair stepped up to the cockpit door, raising his arm to gain access, though the action was needless, as the twins opened the door.

"Doctor Sinclair – how nice of you to visit us again," Serge said, with a hint of sarcasm not lost on Sinclair.

"Please can I sit? I would like to talk."

The stool popped up from the floor as an answer of acceptance.

Alexi spoke in his Muskovian accent. "Please speak freely, Doctor."

Sinclair tensed slightly, sensing that the use of 'Doctor' instead of his preferred Reverend was a sign that work still had to be done to win this duo over to his side, or at least help him.

"Gentlemen. . ." he began.

"No need to be so formal, Gerard. You are amongst friends; at least, for now," teased Serge.

" I will come to the point: I am fucked and I require your help."

"We are listening, Gerard."

"Okay. Ahead is Beatrice 1. You would normally skirt around its surrounding asteroid belt on your way to Space Station 4. I want you to go directly through it." Sinclair eyed the brothers for a reaction. He did not have to wait long for their laughter, simultaneous and loud.

"That would be a dangerous route, Doctor Sinclair, and would only hasten you to your demise on SS4."

"So you could navigate through the belt?" Sinclair asked.

Both Alexi and Serge replied, two Russian voices becoming one,

"We are Space Flyers. We navigate and we fly."

"Do you think AI 131 will attempt it?"

"Maybe; maybe not." Serge replied. "Their craft is smaller, their pilot will take his orders if they are given. You hope to lose them, Doctor?"

"I would pray that that would happen but I am sure they would follow me either way. But – and this is a big but – would they follow us through a Magnetic Dent Portal?"

"What dent?" inquired Alexi.

"Alexi, Serge – I am going to ask you both to take me and my congregation through the dent portal on the extreme side of the asteroid ring, here." Sinclair pointed to the display between the twins. "As you know the time factor is negligible in a portal: you could drop us off in the next solar system and return before the AI ship knows you have used it, then continue on to SS4 and plead ignorance upon arrival."

Again laughter boomed around the cockpit, even for a little longer this time. Then silence. Alexi held up his arm. They were obviously think-linking and did not want to be interrupted. After several moments during which Sinclair grew steadily more anxious and tense, more laughter erupted and then Serge spoke out, his accent sounding more Russian than before, tinged with excitement.

"Okay, Gerard. We shall fly you through the belt and to your portal. We are interested in this adventure. We are Russian military, not a space taxi for religious zealots: your fare will be pricey, more than you can afford, but we will take you, if only for the adrenaline rush of flying the belt."

"Thank you, thank you. I will not forget this."

"Do not worry friend. We will not let you forget." They both replied as the door slid open, the now vacant stool hissing downward.

Magnetic Space Dents were first observed in the outer reaches of our solar system by NASA until, in November 2031, the world received a view much closer to home. The Earth's magnetic belts, known as the South Atlantic Anomaly (SAA), had been fluctuating in their stability over the last fifty years. The Anomaly, being Earth's first line of defence against incoming asteroids and debris, diverted collisions onto the planet's surface by bending the trajectory of such projectiles. However, the strength of the SSA also attracted High Energy Protons, and with the number of satellites in orbit, these protons were causing increasing problems. If an orbiting satellite was struck by a HEP, it could cause a Single Event Upset (SEU) and the impact could short-circuit a satellite causing temporary glitches and often worse. Something had to be done.

Entrepreneur Harold Branson had seen a unique opportunity to not only make some money but to help the global space community clean up some of its own mess. Branson owned and operated a low-orbit space jet, initially catering to the rich and famous but by 2031, flights were more accessible to the public, with larger and larger capacity jets being produced.

Branson had invested millions into Quantum and Solar Sail technology and proceeded to charge the world's governments to salvage their defunct satellites, depleted rocket-fuel tanks and all the recyclable space junk that was circling the globe.

Back in the 1980s, rocket launches would have to wait for weather windows to open up, but by the 2010s there was so much junk orbiting the globe that NASA and the other Space Corporations were risking billions by launching through narrower and narrower windows of opportunity.

Branson Enterprises space salvage operations were opening up huge windows for launches, recovering technology (some of it top secret), enabling the recycling of viable materials and allowing new pathways for the Space Station and Mars settlement constructions. Many countries were glad to have spy satellites retrieved intact and an open orbit to relaunch into. Harold Branson became the world's first multi-trillionaire.

Branson, possessed, ironically, a down-to-earth personality and also contributed to a multitude of diverse charity organisations, providing worldwide aid to the needy.

To astronomers and Howard Branson's amazement, on November 19th 2031 a magnetic dent space anomaly appeared 2.3 light years from the planet Venus. The anomaly was observed for twenty-seven hours and thirteen minutes before disappearing in the black of space. During the twenty-seven-hour period, one of Branson Enterprise's Solar Sail salvage ships lost contact with Flight Operations Control on Earth. For four minutes, all connection and transmission was lost. In the same, exact time frame, the Branson Enterprise

Orbital Space Jet, which was providing a free-of-charge ride of a lifetime to four hundred and eighty-three orphans and their caregivers, sponsored by Howard, lost contact. This four and a half-hour hour, round-the-world trip was to have earth-shattering consequences. Four minutes later, both vessels re-established contact on orbital radar. The QSS salvage ship was remotely guided safely back to Earth but was found to be empty of all its gathered cargo. What was truly horrific was that when the Orbital Space Jet landed, it was also empty; its human passengers, from orphanages across the globe, having vanished without a trace. The five AI cabin crew and the three AI pilots could reveal no explanation as to the whereabouts of the four hundred and eighty-three humans who had been onboard at take-off, their data seamlessly erased.

These inexplicable events essentially ended all orbital space flights to the public. Space, once more, became the domain of governments, warring factions and science.

On the Space Plane, Sarah, one of the Progeny Mission astrophysicists, was still under the effects of the mild sedative Deborah had administered for shock and to combat the added stress from her grief over losing her partner, Anthony. Sarah, a small but plump woman with a short, shiny, black, bob hairstyle, was being comforted and consoled by several members of Sinclair's congregation. Speeding further away from the wreckage of SS2 and the body of her husband only added to her grief and misery. Squeezes, hugs and gentle words struggled to break through the dark cloud of her loss.

Two rows behind, Tasha and Daniel were thanking their lucky stars that they still had each other. Tasha, a schooled geologist, had been testing cosmic rocks and core samples from Mars for over a decade. Her husband and proud father-to-be, was a metallurgist, specialising in temperature fatigue affecting various different metals. His hand, resting on her swollen navel, his ring finger drumming a beat on the dome-like belly of his childhood sweetheart. Daniel Jnr. was kicking back signals of his health and vitality against the womb walls.

"I think he's eager to make an appearance," said Daniel, smiling at Tasha.

"All in good time, Dan. We still have three weeks 'til the due date and I would much rather we were in the medic bay, with Deborah as our midwife, than on this Jump Plane in the middle of nowhere."

Daniel laughed out loud, stating, "SS4 is further in the middle of nowhere." He leant in for a kiss on the cheek. Feeling generous, she let him but the discomfort of her pregnancy and the recent events had left her overtired and more than a little grumpy.

An announcement for everyone to take their seats and secure their harnesses, for approach to an asteroid belt, did little to raise anybody's spirits.

Gerard Sinclair, however, was hoping for a crazy ride, and he was not going to be disappointed.

In the cockpit, the Silchenko twins high-fived and fine-tuned their approach.

AI Bot 131 stared through its optical orbs. "Follow them!" was the only command given.

The auroral light given off by the swirling dust clouds was a good indicator of the frequency of asteroidal collisions. Every ten million years or so, asteroids – some as big as ten kilometers in diameter – would crash into each other and break apart into various sizes and these new clusters, hurling in all directions, were what eventually coalesced into belt systems, so hard to map and consequently to fly through. Even micrometre particles could cause problems for spaceships attempting to navigate a belt system.

Serge released his hand momentarily from his control pad to wipe it on his flight suit: sweaty palms, a sign of the stress the brother pilots were experiencing. Alexi smirked at him, trying out bravado as a release for his stress load.

Small bombs of sand-like particles began blasting the port side of the Space Plane, eroding surface coatings on the exterior panels. The ferocity of the dust cloud was felt in shuddering waves. The exposure felt like being in a hailstorm at a gun range and hoping to come out unscathed. The navigation systems, detecting larger chunks of debris, calculated a winding path that was constantly changing. Golf ball-size chunks pelted the ship mercilessly.

Maintaining a constant velocity, the twin pilots steered past the worst of the maelstrom. Using two forward-facing pulsar thrusters, the boys effectively braked to hold a position behind a larger member of this asteroid family, using it as a buffer against the main swirl of the dust cloud. The clouds formed a pattern drawn towards the sun by its solar radiation. Swinging round this one-kilometre-wide buffer and releasing the braking thrusters, the Space Plane catapulted in an arc towards the inner ring of the belt, avoiding the worst of the rock rain. With minute adjustments on the finger pads, coupled with high-speed reaction times and with the help of the onboard impact predictors, they were taking as few hits as possible. Loud thuds from the tail section of the ship reverberated through all the seat pods before vibrating through the cockpit. Nothing more could be done. Everyone was committed. Up ahead, the magnetic dent anomaly loomed large. Viewed in profile, the dent pulled space and time, bending starlight; Sinclair's only hope for his immediate survival. Amber warning lights on the control panels flicked back to green: they were going to make it, at least as far as the anomaly portal. After that, it was all unknown and uncharted territory.

Simultaneous giggles of relief and anticipation rose from Russian throats: the asteroid belt behind them, ahead the unknown. Smiling and nodding at each other, the twins initiated contact with Sinclair to let him know they had successfully navigated the asteroid belt and were now on approach to the magnetic dent anomaly, his front door to potential freedom.

The AI Bot pursuit vessel was now entering the swirling clouds of the asteroid belt.

Chapter 5

The etherialists' mining recon ship approached the magnetic dent portal, black as the space around it, shaped like two pyramids stuck together, base to base, then slightly elongated. The outer surface absorbed light, the hull offering no reflection; seen only by the absence of the surrounding stars rather than by observing its bulk. It was a mirage more of the imagination than of solid fact. Tall columns supported the interior, with legs spanning out to plateaux forming different floors and bays. Open gantries connected walkways between spacious storage and warehouse facilities holding an assortment of machines intended for testing planet surfaces for future mining operations. There stood three buggies, with six, spoked wheels, on the upper level, a small, test-drilling unit, mounted on a disconnecting frame that could be transported to site and left to take samples. This was parked neatly in the corner of the bay. Various large-volume tanks, containing chemicals and drilling fluids, circled the levels below the buggies.

The recon ship used the dent portals as shortcuts between solar systems and neighbouring galaxies. The flight systems were controlled by the etherialist pilots, remotely, from a homebase on the small planet, Miradon 2710. With no crew on board, all systems were fully automated.

The crew, back on Miradon 2710, had stopped their approach, due to reports of a vessel on the other side of the dent and were awaiting further instructions.

The etherialists' mines and refineries supplied lithium, silicates and marble to alien races spread over seven, connecting solar systems. Earth's Space Planes use a detectable chunk of lithium in their power systems and can easily be stripped and recycled.

Alexi and Serge's Jump Plane was a nice fish in an enormous pond. Nobody should look a gift horse in the mouth and the etherialists were no exception.

The etherialists had no physical body. These entities, alien to earthlings, but widely known to the alien populous of the greater Universe, exhibited a mere smoky presence, drifting wisps of energy or shafts of light, highlighted in different hues, similar to an Earthly sky, constantly changing like chameleons to their surroundings.

Unaffected by time, an absurd concept, these beings, or collection of ions, wafted between liquid, gas and light states, connecting to an intelligence that was outwith solid form but at the same time connecting to solid forms through cosmic vibration, the key to all knowledge.

The Earthly human understanding of 'things', in general, was wrought with misunderstanding and delusion. For the most part, this was due to the build-up of what was known as ego. Ego, for humans, has its place, but like the appendix it serves no function for the greater good and if stimulated in the wrong way, it can have adverse effects on the whole being, resulting in a recycling of molecules and energy.

The etherialists travel star configurations with purpose and are also prone to opportunism. SS2's Space Plane presented an opportunity: their tracking team ascertained access to the Space Planes' computer link systems and realised that the craft was intending to enter the anomaly portal. Guiding the recon ship to the centre and opening the hull bay to receive the incoming plane took but a moment in Earth time. Like a moray eel with its maw gaping, the etherialist ship waited for its quarry.

Using the jump transmission beacons placed between Miradon 2710 and the portal, the signal to the recon ship remained strong, enabling the remote pilots an ease of control.

Serge made another announcement for the passengers to remain in their pod chairs and to have the pod canopies in the raised position. Neither pilot had flown a dent before and the passengers would be safer, and easier to deal with, if they were locked in during any unforeseen circumstances. Serge, being the more charming of the pair, chose to articulate the order as more of a beneficial request. Compliance was ninety-four per cent effective. Sinclair, however, wanted a front-row seat and was heading for the cockpit.

"Doctor – please take your stool and use the harness provided. We do not know what we will encounter once we enter the portal," Serge said as they slowly turned the Space Plane towards the centre of the anomaly.

"Your friend AI 131 and its team entered the asteroid belt, Doctor Sinclair. We shall see how these bots can fly," said Alexi, smirking at his brother.

"We sustained some minor damage – hull and outer shell perforations – but nothing significant," Serge reported proudly. "The security bots will emerge soon. If they make it through, we should enter the magnetic dent portal now. Are you ready, Doctor Sinclair?"

" I am Godspeed," announced Sinclair. "This has to work. They don't call you Russia's finest for nothing, of course."

With the slightest of nods to each other, the twins worked their fingers on the control pads and the Space Plane entered the dent.

Sinclair felt a rush of adrenaline course through his system; surges of hope, clawing at faith. He knew that if they were to succeed in evading the pursuit ship, he would find a planet and become its king. Power would be his, once more.

The inside of the AI pursuit craft was filled with the acrid, blue smoke of an electrical fire. Alarms sounded and lights flashed warnings. This ship and its crew had not been as fortunate in their attempt to navigate the asteroid belt. Significant damage had been inflicted and like a car with a flat tyre, avoiding more damage had been made all the more difficult. The particles in the belt knew no mercy. Still taking hits, AI 131 sat at the monitors, staring only at the holographic image of the Space Plane ahead. It had slowed and made a turn to its right, away from the Brown Dwarf Beatrice 1. Now it was moving again, slowly and on a new heading.

Sparks flew and the sizzle of frying circuit boards filled the small ship, flame retarders blasting at different angles to suppress fire.

"Are we in range to deploy the disabling canons?" AI 131 asked the pilot.

"In thirty-three seconds we will be able to lock on," came the reply, unhindered by emotion.

"Fire now – as a warning. Perhaps they will surrender and cease attempts at evasion."

"3. . . 2. . . 1. . . Cannon blast released," reported the pilot.

The pulsar interrupter beam throbbed on a path toward the Space Plane. Having limped out of the asteroid belt and now in clear space, AI 131 gave the order.

"Prepare to lock on, all cannons."

The Space Plane registered the incoming cannon blast, the warning crystal clear as the monitors showed its approach rendering a visual image of the invisible weapon. The interrupter beam distended and bent as it passed over the entrance to the dent portal, displaying a pull like a black hole sucking up celestial bodies, and then passed harmlessly over the bow of the spaceship. The twins think-linked and before their thoughts could be translated into action, there was a substantial draw felt on the entire ship, accelerating it towards the bright whiteness of the portals centre. The trio of the twins and the flight system combined applied braking systems but no response came. The darkness consumed the ship. There was a total loss of control, the flight computer was mute, the twins fingers drumming unheard beats on the consoles. Electric-blue emergency lighting flickered on; all systems in lockdown, no comms, no flight control, the brightness of the white gate ahead, blinding. The twins pressed back into their seats. Sinclair raised his hands to cover his face. The Space Plane sank into the white doorway like steel melting in a foundry.

The members of Sinclair's congregation and Professor Steed, all confined to their pods, some in pairs, a few solo in their seats, were most busy, fruitlessly pushing buttons trying to ascertain what was going on. Tasha and Daniel were fast asleep, oblivious to everything but their separate dream states.

Deborah Sinclair, wide awake, was holding Sean Steed's hand, the duo flung together by circumstance and captured by placement, had been experiencing not only the physical effects of the ship negotiating the asteroid belt but something strange and alien to them both: attraction. Not black-hole gravitational attraction or magnetic attraction but something, perhaps, more powerful: a soulmate attraction. Neither of them had been exposed to this overwhelmingly powerful encompassment, both busily discussing what was happening, each more excited and baffled than the other as the discussion progressed. Coupled with the outrageous circumstances which they had together endured, very little was understood. Deborah was captivated by Steed's eyes, his alertness, his support and his gratitude for her presence. He, feeling light as a feather, was struck by her beauty, her compassion and her attentiveness. The intensity inside their pod, if harnessed, would have powered the Space Plane to another galaxy.

Breath... heat... then withdrawal. Both had felt it, both still felt it but ideas and thoughts of past and future had already blurred and spoiled the present. Concerns, cares, blocking, at least for now, their freedom to be, to really be. Questions became transparent in their vagueness, feigning interest, replacing the glory of their joy in the moment, when their hearts had collided, open and full. For now, silence was all they shared, their fingers drifting apart.

The AI security ship watched as the Space Plane disappeared, all sensors indicating the plane's non-existence. With power to the drive systems lowered, to accommodate repair and damage control, the pilot was busy balancing optimisations and directing the wounded vessel toward the point in space where the target was last pinpointed. AI 131, its circuits whirring with probable scenarios and outcomes, scanned for the ultimate option available. The dent invited its own version of calculated events: fly in or fly past. AI 131 made the only decision that it could make.

"Follow them," it repeated to the pilot, the bright white centre of the dent waiting, its timeless invitation open to all.

The bot ship felt the tug, swiftly followed by a complete power shutdown, drifting sideways, swallowed by white.

The etherialists guided both ships into receiving hangers 1 and 2, locked them in place, securing them for the journey back to Miradon 2710. The second, smaller craft was seen as a bonus for the bot technology on board.

Sinclair felt the elation of evading his hunters, relief spilling from his tense limbs, the knots of anxiety loosening in his shoulders.

The brilliant white of the portal door, illuminated by the dent's configuration, concentrating bent starlight, had slammed shut behind them. Black, now blinding, their eyes recovering from the white light.

The twins looked at each other in amazement, turning to stare at the jubilant doctor.

"We made it! We are on the other side – turn on the lights!" Sinclair blasted out, bubbling with joy.

"Doctor Sinclair," said Serge, "it appears we have indeed made it through to the other side but we are no longer in control of this ship. We appear to be in a flight bay or a hangar of some sort."

"What?" The colour draining from his face, Sinclair stood and looked out of the cockpit windows. The housing was enormous: tall, grey-black pillars stretched up, blending into darkness; doors, barely visible at the edge of the grey flooring. Nothing moving, silence echoing in the large chamber; minimal lighting casting shadows. "Where are we?"

Laughing in surrender at the situation, the brothers replied, "We don't know, Doctor."

"The Space Plane has been shut down. We are moving but not by our own volition: we are being taken somewhere." Alexi sighed in resignation.

"Where? My God, where?" Gerard Sinclair refilled his anxious mind. His body stiffening with tension, he slouched back onto the stool, groaning into the palms of his trembling hands, his blood pressure skyrocketing.

Chapter 6

In February 2016, Artificial Intelligence took its first faltering steps into the public domain. Under a media frenzy, Hanson Robotics unveiled its AI Robot 'Sophia', its name meaning wisdom, intended to boost regard for this bot's abilities. Sophia toured the globe answering, and sometimes evading, questions; asking questions of her own of famous, credible interviewers, sometimes inspiring awe, sometimes fear, often boredom. The media sensation died down and the public returned their attention to sales at Walmart and their new vacuum-cleaner bot.

The military engaged a different viewpoint, steered towards the applications for death and destruction of their powerful political enemies. It was a movement that did not go unnoticed.

Governments globally joined the race to dehumanise their armies. Drones became bigger and more sophisticated; with remote piloting and automotive bots, being a soldier was rapidly becoming a desk job.

With wars escalating globally, AI Robotics was advancing rapidly, moral concerns ignored through bias on all fronts.

In 2027, a Care Bot had crushed the windpipe of its elderly patient and then proceeded to mutilate the dead body. The media scandal did nothing to curtail advances in AI Robotics. Jobs in the millions were being taken over by autonomous robots. New York proudly opened the first Fire Bot Station, rescues transmitted live on their own television channel. The public consensus about AI technologies spiked and dipped like the stock markets.

Unemployment levels rose steadily: if you weren't making or developing robotics, then you were being replaced by them. Worldwide protests and mass gatherings were being held on all major life-sustaining topics. Riots broke out daily in the most coveted cities, chaos becoming the daily norm.

Aeon 29 was one of the first brands of Security Bot to face the public in the streets. Initially deployed to block streets and protect buildings, these robots were beaten, shot and set on fire. Their protocols soon changed to negate damage, preventative measures implemented, resulting quickly in human deaths. The world was changing in tsunamic waves. Extremes were the environment that babies were born into in the 2030s.

AI Bot 131 was one of the latest versions of the original Aeon 29s. High-end, cerebral algorithms allowed this bot to assess situations and react instantly.

Its exoskeleton was designed for extreme temperatures and pressures of interplanetary space. A polycarbonate epoxy shell covered vital mechanisms, capable of self-repair; a technology in common use on the battlefields raging daily on planet Earth.

The lack of emotion was replaced with a wide range of protocols that motivated AI 131's actions. Reason and logic were justifications to engage protocols and without receiving confirmations or further orders from senior authorities, mission targets were steadily pursued until the resulting capture was acquired.

AI 131 was on a mission: its target, Dr Gerard Sinclair.

"What is our status?" asked AI 131.

"The ship's systems have been locked down. We are in another craft. So far I have not been able to unlock the communication systems: the host ship is travelling to a destination unknown. Without having the ship's systems operational, I cannot ascertain how many lifeforms are on board the host ship or if they are an armed threat," answered the Pilot Bot.

"Can we manually override the door?"

"No, we are being held in stasis by our hosts."

"You two," said AI 131. "Arm your weapons, blast the hinge mechanisms off the side door, on my command. The rest of you prepare to fall into a defensive position as soon as we are out."

The crescent moon dent on the cheek plate of AI 131's face, catching the light from above the emergency door, gave the bot a villainous leer. 131 moved into position with the others.

"Fire."

The two bots looked down at their guns and then at AI 131, their guns mute in their hands.

The speaker in the cockpit sounded with a low whisper, the voice concise and clear.

"We are the etherialists. Your weapons have been deactivated. Your ship is in need of repair. We are transporting you to one of our base planets. Our technicians will repair your ship. You will be free to resume your journey after a short decontamination procedure. We wish you no harm. Your weapons will not function until you return to your own solar system. We will communicate when we land. Stay on board your ship."

The communication ended and the system locked down again. Waiting was the logical option.

"All bots – run a function scan, optimise, then go on standby mode. We wait." AI 131 opened its forearm plate and punched in the code activating the scan. With the scan complete, only the left cheek plate showed an amber warning of damage sustained. AI 131 entered standby mode. An image of Dr Gerard Sinclair remained on the visual file.

The bionic brothers tested the Space Plane's systems; external comms held in lockdown, the internal comms open. Serge made an announcement partially explaining the situation and took a roll call of all passengers, trying to answer a barrage of questions from a confused but uninjured group. The chair pods' hood covers remained locked but provided music and privacy. Serge promised updates as and when they occurred. He and Alexi were now running system diagnostics, where they could gain access. The host ship had taken over the main system and was monitoring what the twins were attempting onboard. Alexi tried the external communication link once more and this time his console flickered with a green light.

"We are the etherialists. We mean you no harm. We are now on route to our base planet Miradon 2710, where you will be quarantined until cleared. There are two life forms attached to their mothers, one of which is soon to arrive amongst you. We will release your seating systems so that you can, if need be, attend to the birth. We will communicate again upon landing." The link went dead and the pod hoods unlocked.

Sinclair went to spread the good news of his communication with their alien hosts and how he had arranged transport to a safe planet for them all.

Deb was snoozing, her head resting on Sean Steed's shoulder. At the click of the pod lock disengaging, she raised her head to gaze into Steed's almond-coloured eyes. A tingling sensation sent goose bumps up and down her body underneath her flight suit. *This man is incredible*, she thought. Sitting upright, she could see her husband touring the aisle. Her swollen bladder made the decision for her. Pressing her palm lightly on Sean's forearm, she said, "I need to pee", giggled then raised her half of the tinted canopy.

Watching her through new eyes, the Professor was spellbound. *What an amazing woman,* he thought, his half-hard cock pressing acknowledgement that his body thought so, too. He leant back, his cock and his forehead pulsing, the pleasure and the pain indistinguishable.

Deborah Sinclair approached her husband, a hostility and a revulsion clawing in the back of her mind.

"What is going on, Gerard?"

"Ah, my dear," his eyes eating up her beauty. "I have arranged us safe passage to a distant planet," he smiled. She looked at him with a puzzled expression. "Please check on Tasha. I had a premonition that Daniel Junior will be joining our flock soon. Please make sure she is comfortable," he said with the air of a newly appointed Pope, then strode off towards his chair pod.

Baffled, she hastened to the toilet with three thoughts on her mind, her bladder, Professor Sean Steed and what scheme her husband was conceiving in his conniving mind.

When she came out of the toilet, she re-allocated water and nutri-packs to her fellow passengers. People were mingling as though they were at a party, gathering in small groups. She caught sight of Sarah, her eyes swollen with tears. They shared a nod before Sarah's look drifted to another place and another time in the past.

Tasha was pacing up and down trying to find some degree of comfort, perspiration glistening on her rose-coloured face. Seeing Deborah she grimaced a forced smile. With sympathy, Deb held her shoulder and examined her belly bump.

"I feel like a sack of watermelons," growled Tasha. A giggle escaped Deborah's scarlet lips. The women hugged, Tasha more leaning than hugging.

"I'm okay," she said.

"Here, keep hydrated," said Deb, handing her a pack of water.

"Take it out on Daniel Senior. It is his fault, after all," Tasha replied, laughing. "It takes two to tango and it was me who asked him to dance."

Suddenly envious of the couple's loving union, Deborah withdrew, thoughts of her own barren womb, unable to house life, echoing in her memory.

"Call me if you need me. We are all right here," she reassured, holding out her arms and swivelling her hips to indicate the interior of the Space Plane, their common situation obvious.

Huddled groups whispered doubts about their destination unknown, their trust in the Reverend Sinclair faltering. 'An alien planet?' 'Why are we not going to SS4?' The recent past wiped their planned futures, replaced them with confusion and rising insecurities. Having faith in the Reverend Sinclair was now creating anxiety, dissolution tearing at the fabric of their beliefs. Life was not going according to plan.

Chapter 7

Sinclair sat in his chair pod, the canopy hiding his shaking body from the others, feeling his own frailty. What was once considered lean was now thin, skinny muscle clinging to long bones. Over the years, since his marriage, his body had begun to fail him, deteriorating with a rotting efficiency. His mind, still sharp, honed by delusions of grandeur, he had been playing the long game: now it was time for a more immediate strategy. Leaning forward, he selected Johan Strauss from the music library and turned up the volume. Adjusting himself into the recliner, he closed his eyes, letting a waltz carry his mind to calm. At least that Security Bot would not find him in this galaxy, he thought, a smile wrinkling his thin face. Pushing his thoughts of AI 131 to the back of his mind, Sinclair dove into the labyrinths of his intellect, searching for a plan to capture the power he had tasted so many years before, his appetite ferocious, starved by neglect. The orchestrated music washed over his mind, calming his anxiety. Glimmers of hope appearing with Strauss's crescendos. If he could only take control of this alien ship, the heavens would be his to navigate. The seed planted, he began to nurture it.

The bionic Russians were discussing their options. They were not happy about losing their connection with their space plane, nor the lack of control. Alexi was doing some stretches behind his flight chair.

"So," he said quietly, hanging upside down and looking at Serge from between his own legs. "What do you want to do about this host of ours, diddling with our beloved plane?"

"Mmm, I have been thinking – if these etherialists can access our control systems, we just have to follow the stream back to the source of the flow. Then, maybe, we can access their systems," said Serge, cocking his head to look down at his brother.

The smile on Alexi's face, upside down or not, was a reflection of his thoughts. "Great minds think alike," he chortled, standing upright again. "We can engineer a by-pass and try to create our own back door into their systems," he suggested.

Serge raised his eyebrows above his sunglasses and spoke. "A door that they cannot slam shut and to which only we have the key." Rubbing his hands together, excited, he leapt into his chair, high-fived his brother and they entered into a think-link session to brainstorm the idea. It would take a balance of deception and caution mixed with the right ratio of courage and conviction. The ability to hide while being observed took great skills. The obvious, they hoped, would blind their watching hosts.

AI Bot 131 was not listening to logic or reason. Effectively being held captive on board this craft inside an alien ship was not logical and not reasonable. With their weapons deactivated, sitting twiddling their robotic thumbs was not an option.

Activating the pilot and the six other Security Bots from standby mode, AI 131 proceeded to inform the bots of the formulated plan. The proposed mission was to gain egress from their pursuit craft, under the floor and through the landing-gear mechanism housing, recon the holding bay and systematically discover the layout of their host vessel. The Pilot Bot was to remain onboard operating external communications and monitoring the team beacons.

The main aim of the small, impromptu mission was to locate and gain access to the flight deck of the host ship; subdue the pilots, take control and use the alien ship to locate, follow and capture SS2's Space Plane that held Dr Sinclair. The task was large and the whereabouts of the Space Plane unknown, but sitting immobile in the belly of this alien spaceship was only wasting valuable time. This to AI 131 was true logic: action towards the end goal was reasonable. The promises made by an alien captor did not compute. AI 131 briefed its team, the finger pad on its robotic hand sliding back and forth along the crescent-shaped dent on its cheek-plate.

Deb Sinclair entered her chair pod, the tinted hood curving over her shoulder as it closed. She met Sean's gaze and moved like a gecko snatching an insect from a windowsill, the speed hard to catch with the naked eye. She straddled his left leg and clutched the back of his neck with both hands, lowering her red-lipped mouth, open, onto his lips. They kissed, tongues exploring lips and gums, darting in and out, mixing saliva, exchanging heat. Deborah ground her hips, her vagina weighing on Sean Steed's leg. His hands wandered immediately, squeezing her waistline in response to her movements, pushing his hardness upwards, his cock straining for freedom, his erection touched her inner thigh. Deborah gasped, pulling her lips from his, a string of mixed moisture trailing from her lip and falling on her chin. Falling back into her own chair, her chest heaving, her head rolling from side to side, mouth open, her back arched. She was close to orgasm. Deb began to relax; her heartbeat slowing, she reached out her right hand towards Steed. The Professor, dazed, aroused and a little confused, took it, lost suddenly in her fingers that lay in his hand, his thumb slowly stroking her knuckles. Swimming in the sensation of his arousal that Deborah had dragged from nowhere to the surface, he was lost in lust. Looking across at her face, he was amazed to see those radiant pools of blue and gold, calmly staring back at him.

Gathering himself with an exhale, like a silent whistle, he sat up and uttered, "Wow. . ." then, even quieter, repeated the word again. "Wow."

Deb reclined for a few minutes, breathing deeply, feeling her body, its reaction noted with heat and dampness, her head felt as big as a football field, light and airy, a room after a spring clean.

"Can we talk, Sean? Like adults?" she added.

"I will try. Here, have some water. Take a minute."

She did.

The chair pod was dark and cool, illuminated only by the glow of the touchpad buttons. Deborah felt, incredibly, at ease. Not shy, not guilty, as though she were reclining on a porch by the beach with a best friend, silently watching the waves crash against the shore. Peaceful.

"That was very passionate, Mrs Sinclair," said Sean, breaking into her private party. She heard Mrs Sinclair at the end and realised it was a call for an explanation.

"I enjoyed it very much, Professor Steed," she replied. " I want to do it again." She let the words hang in the air for a moment before adding, "There is a lot to discuss: my marriage, that kiss, my heart fluttering under my breasts. I can apologise but I am not sorry, so, will you allow me to kiss with you again?" Gliding sideways she faced him, the white of his hair bluish, the black lost in shadow, a shine in his eyes.

Steed leant closer, close enough to hear her breathe, the scent of her hair and skin warm in his nostrils. He reached for her thigh, lowered his eyes for a moment to where his hand touched her leg. She inched closer, her mouth wanting and waiting. He looked up into her eyes and softer than two butterflies dancing, they met again.

Lost and coated in lust, finally they broke apart. Deb opened her eyes and laughed, hearty and free.

"What are you laughing at?" he asked, wanting to join in.

"My husband just marched past our pod. I know him: he has a plan."

Stunned, Sean spun in his recliner and saw the back of Sinclair, his giraffe-like limbs loping towards the cockpit. Steed didn't feel like laughing but when he turned back and saw Deborah, he did feel like kissing.

"Pleased to meet you," he said.

Making little freckled dimples, she replied, "Delighted. It is a pleasure to meet you, too."

Sinclair, ignoring the rest of his congregation, was almost jogging in his haste to reach the cockpit. Expecting the door to hiss open in front of him, he nearly crushed his forehead into it when it didn't. Knocking, he waited, a cloak of desperation shrouding his intent. *Tssh...* The door slid open, the stool rising from the floor; his placement indicated behind the brothers, their heads close, but silent. Sinclair sat, observing the bionic twins, statuesque in front of him.

Separating and turning towards Sinclair, like two mirrors unfolding, their symmetry was startling.

"We are busy, Doctor Sinclair. How can we help you?" said Alexi, his orbital orb zooming in on the doctor.

"You are aware of my situation. I need your help if I am to escape the wrath of Space Fleet: we are all captives of these aliens, the etherialists. I cannot believe that you both are happy with this situation," said Sinclair.

"This situation is not to our liking, Doctor. What are you proposing?" asked Alexi.

"Do you think you can fly this alien ship?"

"We can fly any and all ships, Doctor," the twins boasted together. "We need to gain access to their flight controls, overpower the pilots and crew and bypass any remote links they have to their home base. This we cannot do alone, Doctor."

"Please call me Reverend," suggested Sinclair, irked at the twins' persistence in referring to his sub-alter ego.

A simultaneous, contemptuous laugh burst from the brothers.

"We are not your sheep, Doctor Sinclair, but we suggest that you employ some of your flock to assist in a takeover of the ship in question, and if you can, we will talk once more. If not, do not come to us again. We are formulating a plan of our own for flight control but without your recruitment, we will take our chances with the aliens. Our heads are not the ones on the chopping block," Alexi finished, turning back to his monitor.

Gulping back the slant and the dismissal, Sinclair realised this meeting had not gone well. If the twins were working on a plan to fly this alien craft and he himself could bring them volunteers to assist a takeover, then there was still a slim chance that they all could escape to freedom. *I could be the hero*, he thought.

"I will bring you the help you need. Together we will steal this ship and fly to our freedom," Sinclair announced with as much confidence as he could muster. He stood and left the cockpit to go and charm his disciples.

AI 131 stood above the access hatch to the landing legs, two of his team already crouched on the floor of the bay beneath. 131 waved the next four bots down and quickly followed, landing like a cat, robotic limbs instantly adjusting to the drop and the landing with finely tuned suspension, silently absorbing the stresses. Signalling commands and directions, with sensitive fingers, for the Bot-team to follow. Three pairs manoeuvred out from beneath their craft, the damage from the asteroid belt apparent by the tears and gaping holes in the outer fuselage.

The monotone dark grey colouring of the surrounding walls in the hangar offered nothing but a scale of the enormity of the vessel in comparison to their pursuit craft.

The first sub-team of bots had reached the nearest wall and begun scaling a column that led to several levels above. It was unknown how far these columns rose because of the dim light. Teams 2 and 3 had begun their ascent as AI 131 reached a hangar door with a lockpad on it. AI 131 asked the onboard Pilot Bot for a status update. With no further communications from the aliens yet with solid progress reports from the teams, AI 131 proceeded along the wall to inspect what looked like a window at the top of a small flight of stairs, a possible access to another area.

Team 1 had reached a level and was reporting a description of a pen-like, caged area, possibly used for holding livestock or animals of some kind: there were food and watering units on the walls and evidence of faeces in a drainage grating.

Team 2 were on a level containing six block units, the Pilot Bot monitoring their progress along the gantry, looking for alien lifeforms and heat signatures.

On Miradon 2710, Command ordered the remote activation of level 18 quark-beast electro containment control: intensity factor Yellow.

AI 131 stepped cautiously to the side of what appeared to be a window. Dark shapes and shadow mixed with more distant columns and grey tones. The effect was like looking in a mirror, the adjacent bay identical to this one. Scanning downward and left, AI 131 stood, came out of its crouch and relayed the optical visual images back to the Pilot Bot.

The brightness of the flash behind AI 131 reflected off the window surface, causing the optical sensors to constrict their light uptake. Spinning on the top step and crouching again, AI 131 watched as both members of Team 1 fell backwards and upside down, crashing into the bay floor below with a damaging force. Recalling Teams 2 and 3 immediately, 131 leaped, ten steps at a time, down the stairs towards the crumpled exoshells of Team 1.

An external communication sounded in the security bots' audio systems.

"Our ship can be a danger to trespassers. You were instructed to remain on board your vessel. Recover your belongings and enter your craft."

At this, the main door to the pursuit vessel lowered to the bay floor. Teams 2 and 3 carried the stricken Team 1 Bot aboard, followed by AI 131, the door raised and locked again behind them. Team 1, their circuits fried from the electric-pulse fence of the livestock compound, was laid at the rear of the ship. Without main power, only sections of their exopanels began self-healing, unwrinkling impact creases and attempting to straighten warped connectors.

AI 131 relayed some new information to its crew teams.

"We shall comply with the etherialist demands. There is no longer an urgency to continue the search and apprehension of Dr Gerard Sinclair. The Space Plane we are seeking is in the bay next door." The optical image froze on the Pilot-Bot display screen. "Waiting until we land on the alien planet is the next logical step."

Gerard Sinclair walked up and down the aisle of the Space Plane knocking on pod covers and gathering people together. He stood a good head height over his people, all of them eager to hear what he had to say.

He began. "Loyal followers..." His arms stretched out, "we have come so far together. I, for one, am not going to sit by idly while our captors transport us in this prison ship." The gathered listeners fidgeted and cast sideways glances at each other. "We – together – must take control of this alien craft and I plan, with our pilots, to fly it to our own planet where, *we*, my people, shall ensure humanity survives."

Isaac Goldstein, a man of thirty-three, light, curly brown hair poking out from beneath a NY Giants cap, called from the back of the group.

"What happened to the safety and security of SS4? And humanity surviving on Mars? This sounds like a wild-goose chase," he exclaimed.

"We have no communication link with SS4: it may have been destroyed, the same as SS2; it could have been an attack, perhaps even orchestrated by these aliens!" Sarah shrieked, others gasped. Fear was starting to permeate the crowd.

"What we need is to take over this ship and escape from these aliens. I need some volunteers for an assault on their flight control."

"Not me," said Daniel. "I'm staying right here with my wife. The aliens said they meant us no harm and Tasha is about to have our baby."

"I agree," said Goldstein. "They mean us no harm. They will help us, but not if we piss them off by stealing their ship."

Sinclair could feel the rage and desperation bubbling near the surface of his mind. He could not tackle this task alone.

"The women and the meek," Sinclair paused, eyeing Isaac in the background, "can sit and wait for our victory, but now I need soldiers of the Lord to stand by me in this fight for our freedom. Who is with me?" A demanding tone issued from Sinclair's throat. Mumbles and comments passed between the group.

"Isaac is a coward. That leaves eleven good men. What about you, Professor Steed, or are you going to claim disability with your bionic right arm?" Sinclair watched as his wife's hand went out as if to hold back Steed.

" For your information, Doctor Sinclair, my bionic arm makes my left arm look disabled, so no, I am not going to claim disability. But I see no logic in trying to steal a ship when we have women here, two of them pregnant. Should your plan fail, then we are all sitting ducks."

"Another coward to join Goldstein," blurted Sinclair. "Any more yellow bloods want to cower here while we get kidnapped to an alien planet?" Spittle sprayed from Sinclair's mouth, his steel-grey eyes bulging in their deep sockets. Forging a path down the aisle the Reverend added, "Courage shown in front of the Lord is rewarded with victory. The heroes among us can come see me at my pod; the slaves to cowardice can join the other fools in the queue to Hell."

Stopping beside Steed, he beckoned Deborah. "Come, my dear. Sit with a real man." Steed's bionic arm moved to Sinclair's elbow, applying calculated pressure, enough to see Sinclair wince.

"The lady can choose to sit where she likes," said Steed, releasing Sinclair from the warning.

"I have plans to make: it is better I am alone." The words fell over his shoulder as he lurched towards his seat.

Other pods were already closing, eager to escape the tension. Seven of the younger members of the group were still standing, swithering on the fence of indecision.

Steed watched them from his seat, canopy open, wondering what was going through their minds. How would all this play out, he wondered.

Sinclair knew he had lost control of his emotions, alienating most of his diminishing congregation. The next few minutes would tell how much damage he had done. It was time for prayer.

Half an hour or so later, four young men approached Reverend Sinclair's chair pod.

Professor Steed closed his half of the canopy, sealing himself in next to Deborah.

"Your husband has his soldiers," he sighed. "God help us all."

Chapter 8

Alexi and Serge had spun their chairs around to face the small group that had squeezed into the cockpit. The young men, Tony and Stefano, were good buddies since meeting at MIT, studying to become engineers, both in their twenties, they were in great physical shape; the visits to the gym facilities kept them lean and attractive to the girls involved on the Progeny Mission. Donny and Francis, the brothers suspected, had been cajoled and swayed into their decision to join this group by the two cocky and confident engineers. Donny was a little plump, music being his hobby; sitting at a piano keyboard was his forté and he went to the gym only to walk on the treadmill. Francis enjoyed rock climbing and had lean layers of light muscle showing on his forearms. Francis was a mathematician and an algorithm creator for the space programme.

Sinclair stood between the pairs of recruits, his shoulders slouched towards his chest, stifled by the close quarters of the cockpit and the anxiety crushing down on his mind.

The twins were handing out headsets with earbuds and headcams, while explaining counter measures that they were employing to keep their activities invisible to their alien hosts.

Alexi explained the need to procure a door-activation panel, so that they could build a custom door opener, without which access around the etherialist ship would be impossible.

Sinclair immediately volunteered Francis and Donny.

After audio and visual checks on their headsets, the nervous pair made their way to the side doors of the Space Plane. When the twins had first landed in the bay of the alien ship, Serge had performed a walkaround check to observe the damage sustained from the asteroid belt and to familiarise himself and Alexi with their immediate surroundings. A door pad on the starboard side of the Space Plane was Donny and Francis's target for retrieval.

The two young men stepped cautiously from the Space Plane into the dim light of the holding hangar. The air surrounding them had a coolness, making their flight suits cold to the touch. The odour was slightly metallic, like tasting blood. The door panel was ahead of them to the right of a gigantic column, the top of which disappeared into the darkness above. This vessel was enormous, deep grey tones reminding Francis of standing at the base of a peak in the French Pyrenees before his ascension. The pair moved quietly and swiftly, close enough that the urge to hold hands was strong. Reaching the small square pad, Donny examined how it was attached to the framework. Francis hovered at his side, scanning the enormity of their surroundings for any sign of movement.

Nervous, both men could feel the clamminess of their sweat, clinging in the cold atmosphere.

"I need more light," said Donny. Francis held his flashlight aloft, illuminating the pad.

Watching from the cockpit, the light appeared in the dullness of the bay like firelight in a cave, shadows bouncing with every movement made. An eternal five minutes later, the circle of white light shone a cone on the path taken back to the Space Plane, like a police helicopter chasing a car thief. Francis and Donny appeared in the cockpit doorway, smiles on their pale faces. Donny held the door pad in his hand. Three magnetic connectors hung from the back of the pad.

"Yes!" exclaimed Sinclair, rubbing his claw-like hands together.

Francis set to work with Stefano to manufacture three more hand-held keys, reverse-engineering the existing pad and using the mathematical prowess that Francis brought to the team to unlock and decode the touch pad.

Sinclair busied himself with Serge, trying to figure out how to overcome any resistance in gaining access to the flight controls of the etherialist ship without possessing any arms to combat any lifeforms onboard, none of which had been detected, as yet. Serge and his twin were the only two with any hand-to-hand fighting skills. The conclusion was drawn that the twins would have to split up, Serge and Sinclair forming one team, Tony and Stefano another and Francis and Donny the third. Alexi would remain onboard, coordinating communications and tracking the team's progress throughout the alien ship in the search for the flight control room.

Six mind-numbing hours later, three door pads, plus the original, sat on the console in front of Alexi, a blinking green light on the manufactured pads indicating they were charging.

"I am confident the six-figure code will open the door from the bay but if any other doors we encounter have a different code, which is quite possible, it won't work. I would need to build a scramble decoder for all three pads and that could take days," said Francis.

Sinclair frowned, his hand rubbing the stubble on his pointy chin.

"We have to make do with what we have. Doors of opportunity only remain closed to the unfaithful," he said. "Hydrate. Take some nutripacks. In an hour, we start," said Sinclair.

The young men rose from the floor, scattered with tools and electronics, and filed out through the door. Sinclair nodded to the Russians and followed them out, ducking his head through the door gap, the weight of his skull cracking the top, three vertebrae into place, releasing a fraction of the stress built up; the consequence of his own brash actions.

The six figures paused at the top of the stairs, Sinclair had stopped to take in the sheer size of the hangar into which the Space Plane had been drawn. Serge tugged on his arm, eager to enter the dimness of the hangar bay. The others followed, sounding off, each in turn to Alexi's request for confirmation that the headsets were functioning. Francis reconnected the magnets of the door panel and entered the six-digit code. Immediately the door raised into a slot above. Francis and Donny remained on the bay side of the door as the others passed through. Francis closed the door.

"Okay, Donny. Let's see if our handhelds work," Francis said, holding his crossed fingers up for Donny to see. Donny held the contraption up to the panel and pressed the trigger button with his forefinger. The door raised and the pair stepped through, nudging each other with glee, pride and relief shining in their eyes.

Sinclair nodded and in a quiet voice designated directions and instructions, followed by an order to check-in every five minutes.

The bay they had entered was similar, as far as they could tell, to the one they had just left: large, dark and lifeless. The four walls, widening as they rose, were connected with platforms and walkways. Each team veered off in their appointed directions. Serge and Dr Sinclair smoothly ascended a staircase, the treads made of grating the same shade of grey as the gigantic pillars. Tony and Stefano moved with as much purpose as they could muster, not quite sure what they were looking for, reading glyphs on the walls, with no meaning registering for them. Alexi let them know that their cams had relayed the images and that he was running a cross reference. Donny and Francis, buoyed by their door success, were confidently searching for another door to try.

Stumbling in the dim light, Sinclair was cursing under his breath.

"You should get yourself a bionic orb," laughed Serge, peering back through his sunglasses. "Time to check out our door-opener," he added, standing on the platform next to a single, silver door, next to it a panel with an access pad similar to the bay door. Serge held up his key and pulled the trigger. The door split in two, lengthways, and inside an amber light came on.

"It looks like an elevator."

"After you," said Sinclair, waiting for Serge to enter. Once inside, the doors swished closed. A vertical row of symbols represented the floors. "Alexi?" asked Sinclair.

"I have no idea. I would activate the top one and work my way down from there. It is easier on the legs," he suggested, adding a "Good luck" for good measure.

"It makes sense," said Serge and pushed the uppermost symbol. The small cuboid vibrated slightly, then the doors pulled back to the sides. They stepped out.

Alexi had watched as the two red locator dots rose on his 3-D hologram monitor, extrapolating the numbers. Alexi calculated that his brother and Sinclair had just experienced a two-kilometre elevator ride in the time an artist would take to make a definitive brush stroke.

Gerard Sinclair suddenly felt like he was God again: the view surrounding him and Serge was of galaxies, stars, moons and solar systems not seen before. Serge's optical orbs picked up rivers of infrared flowing through the blackness of space, spotted with colours from milky ways and star constellations. The apex of this craft was a pyramidal observation platform, the walls joined seamlessly to a point ten metres above them. Although both Sinclair and Serge had many months living in space, these new configurations and colours stole their awe and attention. Gerard Sinclair stood, stunned at the possibilities of the Universe in front of him. *I want one of these planets for my own*, he thought, picturing himself overseeing Humanity's future.

"Let's keep moving, boys. We have a flight deck to find," interrupted Alexi.

A single staircase spiralled round the walls into an abyss of darkness, the tops of the giant columns just below them, disappearing from sight, standing from the dark. Sinclair and Serge descended, both briefly looking back up at the stars burning above them. The walls widened beneath them, at a slant; the platforms began to stretch and lead to sub levels. It was eerily quiet; the teams had yet to encounter any signs of life.

Tony and Stefano had been steadily climbing, peering through windows into darkness, occasionally spotting the dim outlines of what looked to be drilling equipment and spare parts for bigger machinery that resembled mining equipment. Their location beacons estimated they were about eight hundred metres below Serge and Sinclair. Alexi informed the two teams that they were nearing the centre of the ship which, from the cams' imaging on the hologram monitor, was taking shape to resemble two pyramids in mirror image; one inverted beneath the other, the centre of the ship being the largest and widest area.

Donny and Francis were exploring the port side of the craft and had entered a transport bay with rows of single-wheeled units plugged into charge ports on the walls.

"These look like fun," said Donny, eyeing the monocycles with boyish joy.

"They look like a crash waiting to happen," said Francis. "Four wheels are tricky enough for me; never mind one."

"What about these then?" said Donny, from further down the line. The scooters had six chairs, one facing the front for the driver; behind that on the left and right sides, facing out, were mini couches with space for two on each side and at the back, a single seat facing to the rear.

"These must be for transporting workers. Where is everyone? We haven't met a single person. It's like a ghostship," said Donny.

Serge and Sinclair met up with Tony and Stefano on a central platform: above them, the towering framework joining to a Starlit apex; below them, through the grated floor, darkness loomed, the dark greyness shading to black. Stefano waved them over to a window port at the edge of the grated platform.

"There is a corridor on the other side with multiple doors. Worth a look, I think. It's the most rooms we have seen so far," he said.

The door panel was further to the right. Serge pulled the trigger on his key and they cautiously entered the long corridor. A lighter shade of grey donned the walls. Intermittently lit by the multiple door panels, it made a welcome change from the gloom behind them. The area felt more used, more purposeful, where perhaps you could encounter personnel or crew. The collective tension of the team turned up a notch. Serge gave some swift, military hand signals and the two pairs split off in opposing directions. Peering through windows and eliminating the closest rooms in the broad corridor, slowly moving further apart, the teams progressed steadily.

Donny was sitting astride one of the monocycles like a child on an arcade bike, hands on the handlebars, racing in his imagination, smiling ear to ear. Francis couldn't help but smile at his joy.

"Unplug me?" said Donny, pointing at the cable leading into the wall. "On this we can cover more ground and find the flight deck quicker, plus my legs hurt," he pleaded through puppy-dog eyes.

"I can't ride that – I've never even seen one before. Let's keep walking."

"Just unplug me. I got this. There's room for two."

Francis gave in and unplugged the monocycle. The screen between the handlebars lit up, one hundred per cent charged flashed on the display, then a lime green line circle appeared on the right side of the touchpad. Smiling, Donny pressed it. The monocycle rose silently, Donny instinctively gripping it with his thighs. Turning the throttle gently, the machine reacted, moving forward away from the wall, turning right towards the door at the end of the line with a simple flick of the handlebars.

"Jump on!" urged Donny through his laughter. Francis swung his leg over, gripping Donny by the shoulder. The monocycle bobbed in its suspended state, adjusting for the additional weight.

"Go slowly, Donny!" said Francis, pleading the order.

"Unauthorised hoverbike activation on Level 57," conveyed the remote controller in the etherialist command centre.

Serge and Dr Sinclair approached a black, glass screen at the end of the corridor they had been exploring. Sinclair looked back along the hallway, the twenty or thirty doors already checked and eliminated stretched into the distance. Dismay sank into Sinclair's hope, the quicksand of despair clawing at his faith.

"Bingo!" said Serge, behind him. "This is it: Flight Control dead-ahead."

Spinning with surprise, Sinclair urged Serge, "It's all clear – go ahead. Can you see anybody?"

"No, no one," replied Serge, raising the key-gun, his finger on the trigger.

Donny and Francis transitioned smoothly from the charging room, the monocycle reacting effortlessly to Donny's input on its controls. As they cleared the doorframe and banked towards the open area between the towering columns, the alarm sirens sounded. Amber lights, sprinkled throughout the ship, spun into flashing rotations.

"What have you done?" shouted Sinclair over the howling of the alarms.

"Nothing yet," confessed Serge, his finger still on the trigger.

"Implement freeze-time stasis," came the etherialist command. "These Earth beings really do have an unbridled passion for curiosity. Maintain Time Freeze on board until our ship is docked. They are close now. Bring it home." The commander hovered in the air, vapours spiralling around his smoky face, a calm misty gaze emanating from his foggy blue being.

Deborah's hand had frozen in time on Sean Steed's lap, his right arm stretched out before him, his eyes shut mid-blink.

Daniel Junior was suspended mid-kick; the tiny footprint protruding, leaving a small hill on the otherwise smooth surface of his mother's belly.

Alexi's head inclined to meet his tattooed hand that was reaching for his earbud. Frozen in time in an instant. His brother was caught staring at his manufactured door key, Sinclair sharing the view at his side, mouth agape, his eagle-nose wrinkled.

Francis and Donny, clinging to man and machine, banked over at a fifty-five-degree angle, suspended by an invisible force six hundred and fifty metres above a visible deep, dark void.

The entire ship was caught in one slice of time. Alarms were silenced, now peacefully navigating the last leg of the journey to Miradon 2710.

Chapter 9

On the ground a large, flat square slid sideways revealing the docking pyramid, inverted to accommodate the base of the etherialists' recon ship. With incredible precision the ship lowered and locked in place, seals expanding to keep dust and creatures from fouling the mechanisms below. From the surface, with the top half of the ship protruding from the ground, a perfect black pyramid stood, reaching to the orange of the sky above. Two other pyramids sat majestically in their docks. All that was missing was a sphynx: the similarity to the Great Pyramids of Giza on Earth was indisputable. Remarkable.

Flight systems shut down, underground teams of etherialists travelled on transport buggies to board the spacecraft. Interconnecting tunnels sloped gently to each level, a massive termite system of organisation.

Bay doors hissed open all over the ship, like an Italian woman opening windows on a spring morning, allowing the teams access to all the subsurface levels. Once the welcoming teams were in place, the Time Freeze system was deactivated.

Francis and Donny got the biggest shock, hanging in mid-air, half a kilometre of platforms and gangways below them. They were held in suspension under each arm by two bluish apparitions. Letting out a yelp, Donny struggled against fear, his legs walking as if treading water in a swimming pool. He was shocked further when the blue smoke that was supporting him spoke, whispering, "Please, come with us."

Led by the four vaporous shapes, Donny and Francis were safely placed on a platform, outside the monocycle-charging facility, where through a window Donny could see the borrowed hoverbike being plugged back into the charging wall by what looked like a figure of cigarette smoke. Joy rippled through their bodies, the pleasure of standing on something solid and substantial, overwhelming. Even for Francis, the thrill he enjoyed and sought, dangling from a rope on a mountainside, was incomparable to the gratitude he now felt to his rescuers from over the abyss that he had woken to seconds before.

Serge and Sinclair gasped at the smoke before them, surrounded on all sides without fire.

"Aargh!" Sinclair cried out, when a voice wafted from the mist in front of them.

"Please come with us. You are being taken for decontamination," the voice had said. Their arms felt a pressure as a blue wisp curled around them, leading them down the corridor away from the unopened glass door. Their footfalls lighter on the floor, a floating quality to their step.

The passengers on board the Space Plane were being guided towards the transport buggies, many with pale, confused faces.

Tony and Stefano had been a little more reactive when time had resumed. Their last memory had been alarm sirens wailing, then their first response to finding themselves surrounded by blue smoke was to run, hampered by the smoke itself holding them in place. A vigorous struggle had ensued. Both men were now kneeling, hands behind their backs, white straps of light binding their wrists, their foreheads against the wall of the corridor. Panicked and subdued, their minds struggling to hear the calm voice of the blue wisps asking them not to resist, the sight of Sinclair and Serge, almost floating towards them in a cloud, did nothing to help them understand their immediate circumstance. Gently lifted to standing, the two groups met and were led, as one, to an awaiting transport buggy. Seated, the light-cuffs puffed from existence, releasing Tony and Stefano's wrists. The buggy accelerated forward, leaving the ship and entering a well-lit tunnel, the driver's blue tendrils of fumes, flowing like long hair in the wind with the forward motion.

Kalianne Devaroux released her finger from the winch button, the cold clear water spilling over the rim of the well bucket. She watched as the black ship hung in the orange sky above its mooring, before descending into its docking station, home from another exploratory mission. Transferring the water to her earthen carry jug, she turned, heading down the worn, clay path to her house, her indoor plants in need of the water. Yellow and pink flowers burst from purple pods at the side of the path in her wake, the flowers re-emerging, having retracted with the vibrations of her approaching steps when she had passed towards the well. Her garden, mostly wild, was kept mainly for the mix of colour it produced. The main cultivation plot of the commune still produced more than enough fruits and vegetables for everyone. Kalianne preferred to cultivate colour. The orange and pink hues from the two moons, salask and empere, were dimming as they set behind the hills, the jagged ridges stretching like a naked spine across the plains. The night sky here on Miradon never darkened, lit by a third moon Amethysia, the largest of the three moons, pouring violets and purples over the landscape. The orange glow from salask always deepened just before the moonset; it was Kalianne's favourite colour, the same as her flowing hair. Kalianne was one of several hundred of the human villagers who lived and shared the planet with the etherialists. Some of the menfolk worked at the marble mines in the distant hills. There was no necessity for it: the village provided everything that was needed for a comfortable existence. It was thought the men simply enjoyed riding on the huge machines, the pleasant mountain air and the time spent away from the community. They would go and return as they pleased.

Miradon 2710, a slow, rotating planet, its atmosphere a constant ten degrees Celsius, warmed by its molten core. It cooled a degree every hundred thousand years, so in a mega-annum the surface lakes would freeze, but for now the humans found it habitable.

Trees and plants, some of which the etherialists brought from other star systems, flourished in the village gardens and fought for control over space in the gullies of the hillsides.

Mammals, like the quark-beasts, were domesticated, kept by the villagers for their under-pelt and milk and used by the etherialists for hauling test equipment on terrain too steep for their buggies, their six powerful legs being put to full use. Larger, wilder beasts were kept away from the village and mining areas by force fields erected by the etherialists, sonic defenders inaudible to the humans. The gravity on Miradon, less than Earth's, produced a lightness to movement felt by the first settlers but unnoticed by those who were Miradon born.

Serge and the other three exited the tunnel under a blood-orange sky onto a dusty, clay road leading to a large, smooth, windowless building the colour of slate. To their left, in the dip below, a herd of large animals munched on huge purple leaves growing from the clay soil. The quark-beasts stood on six clawed feet, dragging a thick tail behind from below their shelled backs: a domed carapace three metres tall, plated like a car-sized turtle. One of the creatures stood up on its hind legs, its fore feet leaning on the fence cable, long toothy claws curling in between the gaps, its smooth underbelly, squares like paving stones, each with a fist-sized teat in the centre of the crème-coloured sections. They had eight nipples, in all, to accommodate their brood. The long pucia-coloured hair that hung from below the shell was dreadlocked with clumps of clay. A horn blast sounded from its open mouth, whistling past tusks and teeth, purple saliva dripping on the fence cables.

The etherialist driver paid no attention but the four new arrivals instinctively leaned away from these massive mammals.

Beyond the corner of the pen, Sinclair was trying to make out what looked like clusters of low buildings built using stone and the surrounding clay, the colour blending into the environment. His attention was drawn back to the contrasting slate grey of the building into which they were being driven.

Deborah Sinclair and Sean Steed shared a transport buggy with Tasha and Daniel. Deborah, feeling the movements of the baby inside Tasha, surmised his arrival was imminent sooner than the expected due date. *Not surprising*, she thought, *with all the excitement going on.*

A train of six buggies waited in line as the last of the passengers disembarked the Space Plane, escorted by the blue and white mists of the etherialist forms. Alexi sat alone in the last buggy, shouldered by turquoise vapours. The buggy train moved off up the slope of the tunnel. Alexi looked to his left as they exited the ship: in the adjacent tunnel he glimpsed another buggy. Their optical orbs met, AI 131 and three other bots, their buggy slipping into a tunnel. The Space Plane had been followed through the magnetic dent.

The sky was turning a reddish violet, Amethysia rising over the southern plains as the last pinks of empere reflected on the hills beyond the valley. People in the village were gathering at its centre, a flat-bottomed bowl forming an auditorium, where plays, storytelling and village meetings were held.

Kalianne was the village scribe, taking over the role from her mother who had died five years previously. A heart attack had taken her quickly. Now the stories of the village, both historical and current, were written and stored by Kalianne. She used a touchpad to capture the spoken word and all data was stored in the main hall. Her favourite part of recording was the use of a mabrial feather for a quill and beetsap juice, bled from a bush in her garden for a quick-drying ink, enabling her to scribe by hand the books for the village library records.

Word had reached the village that humans had been on board the last recon ship to dock. It had been twenty-one years since the village originators had been brought here, when the etherialists had plucked an orbital jet from its flight path, along with a Branson Enterprise Solar Sail Salvage ship, scooped for its cargo. Four hundred and eighty-three humans had been aboard the low-orbit jet and were the founding fathers of the Miradon 2710 Bio-village. Kalianne was one-year old.

The human colony had thrived, the etherialists had wanted to study the auric bodies of the earthlings, the orbital jet providing a broad age range of both sexes. The studies were harmless to the human subjects, many in fact enjoying the probing of their auric layers.

It was quickly understood that there would be no return to planet Earth and a new energetic verve for life emerged, free of war and familiar struggles. Creativity and ideas pulsed with communication and freedom. Organisation and construction had, at first, been stumbling blocks to hurdle, the etherialists gently guiding them through initial transitions, leading them to believe in themselves. The four hundred and eighty-three humans took their first essential steps towards creating a viable, mesmerising, organic unity, simply called 'The Village'.

The etherialists provided protection, freedom and help. The colony flourished with collective wisdom, the melding of ancient and modern giving birth to the contentment of living in the now.

The possibility of more humans arriving on Miradon 2710 had stirred an immense amount of speculation. A meeting had been called at the auditorium for after moon-set, with all to attend.

The decontamination hall resembled a large car wash. Stripping naked, the passengers deposited their flight suits into chutes and placed their footwear on a thin conveyor belt that ran parallel and ahead of them. Stepping through a wall of fine mist, the passengers were then sprayed completely, liquid jets scouring every and all areas and orifices. Emerging, their bodies tingling and spotless, they travelled through the driers and passed the body scanners and chip readers. Several etherialists hovered at the end of the hall, handing out soft tunics made from quark-beast wool and then leading the new arrivals to a spacious waiting area on the right.

Deb Sinclair and Sean Steed were the last of the group to strip down, Deb catching Sean averting his eyes from a stolen peek at her naked behind. A smile curved on her ruby-red lips.

"Please – after you," he gestured with his bionic arm, silently hoping the mist wall was cold.

Sinclair, Serge and the four young men were led into the decontamination hall. Sinclair, looking over the group, had seen his wife, with Professor Steed's hand on the small of her naked back, and then they were gone, swallowed by a curtain of fog. Irritated, he kicked off his boots and removed his clothing, falling in line with the others. A pair of sunglasses sticking out of flight boots wobbled out of sight on the conveyor belt.

Dressed in the smooth robes the light beings had given them, they were led past a plush suite where the rest of the passengers could be seen talking and drinking hot beverages, some reclining on plump cushions. The etherialist guides ushered the six into a smaller, windowless room, the only furniture being a long bench running down the length of one wall. The door slid closed behind them and clicked.

AI 131 and the bot team – two of the bots lying incapacitated on hovering tables – were brought to a mechanical facility where the two bots, their circuitry fried, were left on the tables. AI 131, the Pilot-Bot and the rest of the crew were then led through the decontamination hall. With no need to remove any clothing, they stepped through the mist wall. The etherialists downloaded the cerebral data from each member and then, passing a locked door on their left, entered the neighbouring room, stood by the long single bench and watched as the door slid closed, a faint click emanating from the panel.

Sinclair swirled as the door opened. Silhouetted in the doorway Alexi entered, his two optical orbs shining as they came to rest on his brother. The door clicked behind him as they hugged. Releasing Serge from his embrace, he stepped toward Dr Sinclair.

"Take a seat, Doctor. I have news for you."

Chapter 10

The village inhabitants slowly gathered at the auditorium; a circular pit which rose majestically, terraced with curving stone benches, a gladiator ring without the bloodshed. Lit by the violet light emanating from amesthysia, the stones glowed with the warmth of the heated debates of the past.

Martin Norrell, the chair of the committee, called for attention at the opening of the discussions, an action administered to hush the crowd's excited gabblings. Martin was a tremendous compère with the ease and command of an effective orator. His background was the theatre and the role of captivating an audience filled him with delight and purpose. His dark-bearded mouth projected the words so that all could hear and the motion of his eyes as he spoke included everyone personally in the topics up for discussion.

Kalianne sat to the side, left of centre, her touchpad ready beneath her poised fingers. She wondered, as the crowd settled, how the arrival of the newcomers to the planet would affect the village.

Martin Norrell informed the crowd of the report he had received from the smoky apparition, Offimus, the main liaison between the village and the etherialists, then opened the floor for opinions. The village baker, Martha, was the first to speak, her high-pitched voice rising from the back of the crowd. Still covered in a light dusting of green flour, used to produce her delights, she stood and spoke without concern.

"I think it will be wonderful to hear news of home. Much will have changed – of that I am sure. I suggest that we welcome these people with open arms and open hearts." At this, she sat her ample buttocks back down onto the smooth stone of the bench. A few claps of agreement rippled through the crowd but were halted by Jonathan Miles standing and offering his opinion.

"Martha is romanticising thoughts of Earth. When we left, chaos was the order of the day. I can't see it having improved in these last years. We have it good here – our own slice of heaven. We should be cautious of the newcomers." Murmurs and heads bobbed in small comments with neighbours. Jonathan continued,

"It will not be easy for them to give up hope of a return to Earth, as it was a difficult transition for us. I suggest we offer support where we can but I advise alertness against troublemakers to our peaceful existence. Let us not forget the religious sect." The reminder caused comments to fly off a louder vocal chorus, until Martin stepped in to restore order.

"Please, these points are valid and everyone shall have a say but Kalianne can only scribe one voice at a time. We have much to discuss; a consensus must be met," he said, nodding his support to Kalianne who smiled a *thank you* in return. The meeting continued for some time longer until the suggestion of a break was met with raucous applause. The deep violet of the sky had begun to redden by the time the meeting was concluded, the tangerine halo of salask signalling the imminent moon rise.

It was decided, unanimously, to welcome the newcomers with hearts full of love and to assist the etherialists in the construction of the temporary shelters. The village planner left the meeting, excited at the prospect of designing functional additions to the village footprint. The overall feeling from the community inhabitants was of warmth and eagerness, a peculiar reunion of strangers.

Alexi had broken the bad news about the AI-Bot pursuit team following them through the dent portal and them being on the same alien ship as the one they had all just left, suggesting the obvious: that it was only a matter of time before Dr Sinclair and AI 131 were to have another close encounter. Alexi had not meant to deliver the news so succinctly and after the Doctor had collapsed to the floor, realised the employment of some tact might have resulted in a less dramatic outcome. The others had banged on the door when Sinclair had lost consciousness. Two, misty, blue clouds had entered and taken him away.

Gerard Sinclair was taking thiazide, an antihypersensitive; a treatment for his high blood pressure. His supply was crushed in his room on the crumpled space wreckage of SS2. Floating in the neighbouring solar system had left his physical being at a disadvantage. Sinclair's health had been in a downward spiral for years. Nine months after his marriage, he had been hospitalised with palpitations of the heart and a baffled doctor told him that he was sterile due to the large quantities of progesterone found in his bloodstream. Gerard Sinclair was struggling mentally with his own increasing bouts of impotency and revealing any personal details to a fellow doctor was beyond him. A dark shadow of depression clawed persistently at the secrets he chose to withhold. His wife, bearing the news of his sterility and already in the know concerning his impotency, stood beside him, sworn to secrecy, of course, citing, "I didn't marry you for your manhood but rather for your intellect." This had brought a smile to Gerard's grey pallor and set his mind at ease but it still did not answer the question of how the sterilisation drug had entered his system.

Sinclair woke up in what was obviously a room in a hospital or a clinic of some kind. An etherialist hovered at the foot of the bed, shimmering in the bright light.

"You are showing signs of hypertension. We will medicate and sedate you until the present danger to your wellbeing has passed," it said, the words coming in puffs, like smoke rings, from its steamy mouth. A liquid pump whirred by Sinclair's bed as the sedative entered his vein.

The etherialist Offimus visited with Martin Norrell two moon-sets after the village meeting. The dialogue between them had always been amiable and concise. The etherialists were consistent in their aid to the village, listening to ideas and imparting knowledge in response. Martin told Offimus of the village's decision to welcome the newcomers with love and openness. He did not mention that a small number of the community held a few concerns as to the smoothness of the integration, as he felt that this could be handled within the community. Offimus announced that temporary shelters would be erected and indicated an area by the river that was suitable.

"We shall let your village planner decide upon a more permanent location for new dwellings," Offimus replied, adding, "We can sense his excitement."

Martin had long since accepted the strange powers that the light beings possessed; knowledge of emotions felt rather than voiced. The etherialists were like mind readers. Communicating on a human level was far below their capacity; it was baby-talk and base. Martin said some of the villagers would be delighted to help with the preparations, although instinctively he knew that Offimus already felt this. Offimus dipped his smoky head in a bow of acceptance and floated towards the buildings on the ridge above the village.

Offimus entered the plush waiting room, all heads turning. A silence fell upon the room.

"Welcome to Miradon 2710." Light wisps curled into the air.

Isaac Goldstein stood up from the cushion in the corner.

"When can we return to our ship?" he asked. "We come in peace and mean you no harm." A blast of light burst from Offimus like a solar flare, accompanied by the sound of joyous laughter.

"This is your new home. Miradon has a human colony that eagerly awaits your presence." This news brought gasps from the room, quickly subdued by Offimus stating that there would be no return to the gathering's home solar system. Interrupting the buzz of conversations, Offimus raised a translucent arm, signalling for quiet.

"I shall return promptly to explain your new situation, to answer all questions and to inform you what is expected from you all, but first I must ask for your patience." Swirling to the right, a white finger, steaming like an icicle, pointed to Tasha. "Please bring your husband: you are about to become a mother."

Tasha, leaning on the counter by the water dispenser, turned towards Daniel, her expression full of emotion, excitement, fear, panic, surrender, doubt, and then she felt it: her tunic soaked below the waist, her womb waters ran over her bare feet, puddling on the floor. A cramp seized her pelvis and a moan jumped from her throat.

"Please come with me. Your baby boy is eager," Offimus stated, the tone compassionate, ringing with understanding. Deborah leapt to Tasha's side, supporting her arm, Daniel taking her other arm, and they led her to the door. A bright blue smile led them through the corridor. Voices competing to be heard were left in the luxurious chamber behind them.

"We come in peace," said Steed, as he sat down next to Isaac. "Did I really say that?"

Both laughed nervously, releasing some of the tension that hung in the air.

Tasha, Daniel and Deb entered a bright, octagonal space, doors on five of the eight walls. A bed, perforated with tiny holes, hovered next to a wall windowed with monitors. Six etherialists floated into the room as Offimus exited. Tasha's damp tunic was removed and replaced with a small jacket of the same material: it bore flaps over the chest secured with two small buttons. The table felt slightly warm beneath her, lowering as she sat and then rising to waist-height as she lay back, a cushion of air blowing gently beneath her shoulders and head. The smoky attendants spoke softly, their voices reassuring. A glass of water and a small red tablet was offered.

"What is that?" asked Deborah.

"To ease the pain of the contraction cramps, a natural product coated in an edible shell, also natural. There is no need to worry – the birth will go well."

The voice, incredibly persuasive in its delivery, left Deborah only nodding for Tasha to take it. Daniel stood to Tasha's right, holding her hand and blabbering encouragement, Deborah monitoring and measuring dilation. Four of the light beings left, leaving two pushing buttons and twisting dials on the monitors.

Another cramp squeezed Tasha, her fingers crushing against Daniel's finger bones. It was he who let out the yelp.

"Don't push yet, Tasha: a few centimetres to go," Deb said, not looking up from between Tasha's legs. The pill had taken its effect and the contractions softened, feeling more like regular menstrual cramps than the powerful cramps associated with labour. The two ladies looked at each other, both more worried now about Daniel who looked comically like a fish out of water. One of the attendants slid a chair behind Daniel, his body accepting it without recognition.

Two of the etherialists returned. It struck Deborah that she could differentiate between the luminous beings: each had its own pattern of movement, the light and smoke different but the same, forming individual fluidity of movement forming distinctive colour patterns.

The nearest spoke. "You can push gently and gradually with the next contraction." Tasha looked to

Deb for confirmation. Deb examined the area thinking *How do they know this?* All evidence was that, indeed, it was time: dilation ten centimeters; Daniel Junior, lying the right way; mother focused, father blank-faced, his mind racing with abstract thoughts.

"You ready, Tash?" asked Deb in acknowledgement. A ripple of pressure shuddered from the back of Tasha's neck down to her heels that were firmly lodged in the corners of the hovering bed. Daniel Junior was on his way.

With a final squeeze, Daniel Junior's feet appeared while Deborah supported the baby's head. Light-blue arms took over, a hand offering the proud father a laser tong. Daniel Senior fingered the trigger and the umbilical severed: a clean precise cut. A basin was wheeled to the side of the bed, and the etherialists washed baby Daniel. Tasha pushed out the afterbirth, pulling Daddy close for a kiss, partially for the distraction to allow this unusual birthing team to focus on the clean-up. An attendant offered the baby to Tasha just as a wail from baby Daniel brought smiles to the faces of all. As she unbuttoned a breast flap, tears rolling down her cheek, Daniel Junior's lips latched on to his mother.

"Thank you," she said, staring into aqua-blue eyes, shining.

"You are welcome. Your son has a pure aura and will grow to be a fine man: we have seen this. At the second moon-set, you can return to your comrades as a family."

At this, they left the octagon, the lights in the room dimming slightly.

"Moon-set?" said Daniel and they all laughed, joyous in the moment, Deborah swallowing a past bitterness that every birth awoke in her.

Gerard Sinclair lay sedated in a room further down the corridor, his eyeballs flitting from side to side in REM state. In his lucid dream, he had just reached the apex of a rocky ridge. Below him, where the boulders and scree stopped, a thick forest of trees began. He slid the short distance down and entered the forest. The tall trees, with trunks too big to hug, were covered in a rust-red bark striped with silver bands spiralling upward to the first protruding boughs. The silver became more prominent, the higher branches showing little of the trunk's russet hues. Copper-orange leaves blocked out most of the violet sky. Sinclair's subconscious picked up the feel of the cool breeze, his own arm coming into view as he touched the tree, his palm print shining silver where the outer bark fell away, crumbling beneath his touch. A path formed by the roaming creatures of the forest angled downward to his left, his decision whether to follow it made easy by the uninviting undergrowth to each side. Exhausted struggle and urgency became the backdrop of his dream state, seeking shelter, his goal. Moving off quickly, his body then came to a sudden halt at an intersection on the trail. The fork to his left continued downwards, through thick trees; to his right the track levelled off, leading to and from an overhang of large boulders, the mouth of a cave, dark in a recess of the hillside. Sinclair moved cautiously towards the black of the cave entrance, the sand in front, smooth from wear. His right hand came into his dream vision, his body stooping, his hand gripping and throwing a small rock into the blackness. After the echoes of the bouncing rock faded, only the rustle of the leaves in the canopy above dominated the silence. Sinclair moved forward, eyes straining into the darkness.

As Gerard Sinclair turned in his bed, the pump beside him gently whirred into action and the bright blue wisp left the room.

Alexi and Serge paced the room, turning in unison every twenty steps. The other four watched them from the bench like spectators at a tennis match. Think-linking was generally a silent process but Tony could hear the occasional sigh and could see expressions of emotion coming and going on the faces of the twins.

"I need to piss really badly," said Donny, restless and fidgety on the bench. "When the– What the hell?" he exclaimed as a pipe snaked its way from the floor like a cobra from a basket.

"Go ahead," laughed Francis. "Maybe if I say I could do with a massage, a magic table and a Swedish blonde will appear. . ." Sniggers filled the room. Donny approached the pipe, its corrugations stiffened and a light suction commenced.

"Don't get sucked in there," joked Stefano. While the others giggled, eyebrows bouncing, bringing more laughter, Donny nervously relieved himself, glad of the opportunity.

"How long are we going to be in here?" he complained. No one answered. The twins paced shoulder to shoulder.

Next door AI 131 and its team lined the bench in power-saving mode. Silent, identical manikins in hibernation.

Offimus opened the waiting-lounge door to the gaze of the human occupants. Two etherialists wafted in behind him and parked a trolley of flight boots, neatly labelled with name tags, next to the water dispenser. Smiling through a hazy, light beard, he motioned with his arm towards the trolley.
"Please select your own footwear. We are about to embark on a short walk to the village and your temporary accommodation." Words puffed in streams of light rays.

In the light under a salask sky, Offimus's blue body stood out against the orange, the corner wall of the dark building, visible through his body.

The human snake, two and three wide, walked on light feet, bouncing with the lesser gravity, following Offimus to the edge of the ridge path above the village.

From above they could make out the spiralling layout, its centre reminding Isaac of a bullring he had visited once in Spain. Single-storey buildings curved in a Fibonacci pattern out from the centre, widening outward from the dip in the landscape. On the far side of the village ran a river, its source from the hills beyond. On flat ground, over the river, a series of larger buildings stood; it looked like a lumber yard full of silver-coloured wood. Large, six-legged beasts moved loaded trailers between the buildings.

Well-worn, clay pathways circled throughout the village; small streams passed under miniature bridges. The air was cool but the orange sky gifted a psychological warmth. Smoke could be seen rising from a few chimneys below, quickly dissipating in the light breeze.

Six men and two women approached the group as they neared the edge of the community.

"Welcome, welcome!" said a tall, broad-shouldered man with a bushy, black beard. "My name is Martin Norrell – we are delighted to greet you."

Martin nodded an exchange with Offimus, the handover apparently executed. Both groups shaking hands; introductions and conversations, some concerned, some excited, rose from the mingling hoard. Martin led the way to a row of geodesic domes, more villagers bringing blankets and containers of water. Indigo patties the size of small books were being stacked outside the domes, Martin explaining to the curious faces that dried quark beast dung was used for fires and smiling, almost proudly, saying the aroma given off was actually rather pleasant.

Empere, rising close behind salask, added its pinkish hue to the orange light as the newcomers began to settle in.

Sean Steed squatted outside at the back of his dome, his eyes taking in the reflection of the two moons on the steady flow of the river water. His mind, a torrent of thoughts, flooding and obscuring reason. Deborah Sinclair was a fountain of joy, his heart a boulder, awash with the passion of her waterfall.

Chapter 11

The Ethereal Captain of Flight, Merchantim, carried himself in a darker, denser, blue-black body, fading to deep blue at the outer edges of his floating being. His eyes, however, shone bright, light azul beads staring from their midnight-dark surroundings. He viewed the AI bots as they activated and stood up from the bench.

"You are not in protect mode; you are hunting and seeking," said Merchantim with no introduction. AI 131 stepped forward.

"Yes, we seek a man to answer for his actions that led to the possible and likely demise of others."

Merchantim floated closer, AI 131 tilting its head back to look into the alien eyes.

"Your pursuit is over," Merchantim continued. "We have your man in our care. There is no need for you to continue the hunt."

"This man must be brought before a judicial committee. He acted in a—"

"Please follow me," interrupted Merchantim. The door opened, the ethereal captain leading the way. Moving like a flag in the breeze, the captain ushered the bot team into the mechanical facility. The two fused bots still lay on the hover tables, their face and chest-plating set off to the side, their damaged circuitry being removed. As Merchantim spoke, tendrils of near-black smoke wafted beneath his eyes.

"You are in need of a charge, please step up to the finger ports on the wall." His arm indicated the wall to his left.

"I shall return when you are fully charged," whispered Merchantim. The bots lined up. AI 131 issued the order to remain alert, then they connected to the charger ports. Merchantim streamed over to the technicians working on the disabled bots.

"Prepare them all for transportation to Blandar."

The village pub was packed, inside and out. The buzz of conversation was audible from outside the bakers, which was several paces around the curve of the broad pathway. Donny and Francis were tasting the delights produced by Martha while she, giddy with excitement, busily made innuendo about her buns, eyeing Donny, the target of her advances.

Martin Norrell and some of the other village men sat with some of the newcomers, the tables in the pub full of pottery mugs brimming with the local brew. Green froth rimming mugs and moustaches alike, nicknamed grale (short for green ale), the beer was tasty and powerful. The same green wheat that Martha used as flour in the bakery went into the production of the grale and grew on the plains between the lumberyard and the foothills.

Some of the ladies were being introduced to the wine, made from the separg vine, cultivated in the village vineyard.

Stories from the inception of the village competed with news from the space stations and planet Earth. Eruptions of laughter bounced off the thick stone walls. Sobs and hugs interspersed with the jovial moments until, finally, Tom rang the chimes from behind the bar, calling for last orders in the momentary silence. A loud roar of laughter followed by applause erupted when Isaac asked for the bill and was told that money did not exist in the community. After the applause from the newcomers had died down, Martin stood and addressed them all.

"We have no need for finances here on Miradon," he said, full of pride, adding, "We all chip in and help with the workings of our home here: we and you shall want for nothing. Amysthesia is high in the sky now, when empere joins salask, we will meet in the auditorium to discuss the plans and assignation of crews for the construction of your new dwellings. It is thirsty work so, speaking for myself, I am ready to hydrate with a final mug of grale, if you please, Tom."

Martin sat, enjoying the smiles shining from the faces of the humans at the table in front of him.

Slowly, in small groups, the gathering cleared, some showing signs of the effects of the grale, swaying under the violet sky.

Gerard Sinclair had opened his eyes and seen his wife staring at him through the window of his room. His body felt stiff and drugged, his eyes closed and the forest appeared; he could not feel the heat of the small fire in front of him, silver sticks flickering at his feet. A fine mist filtered through the trees in front of the cave. A mabrial flew on to a bough below, its wings spreading just before landing revealing a fuchsia underbelly, orchid-pink feathers, spotted with plum-coloured speckles, its broad back tapered towards a tail the same orange as the surrounding leaves. The mabrial looked at him through the flames, a shriek hung in the mist before echoing in the cave. Sinclair took in the stare, acknowledging the hooked beak and the sharp talons that dug easily into the bark of the tree. With a powerful hop, the majestic bird of prey leapt from the bough, dropping through the forest, wings spread, mist curling in its wake, silently gliding in its departure. Sinclair's dream hand laid the last stick of the pile on the glowing embers.

When he opened his eyes again, his wife was no longer at the window.

It was under a coral-coloured sky that Deb, Tasha and the Daniels came over the lip of the amphitheatre.

Daniel Junior was swathed in a quark-beast blanket, smiling up at the moons, content in his mother's arms. Below them, the curving benches were filled with groups of construction crews listening and relating to plans.

The beaming parents were met on the steps by a small group of doting admirers,. "Oohs" and "aahs" reached Deb's ears as the new family was ushered aside onto one of the curving stone benches, baby Daniel being passed around. Deborah's ears closed as her eyes opened wide at the sight she had been scanning the crowd to see: Sean Steed. An excitement thrilled through her as she descended the wide steps towards the group. The gathering of men stood, readying to depart the auditorium, their tasks set. Deborah approached from behind, admiring Sean's broad shoulders, the purple tunic setting off his dark skin and salt-and-pepper hair.

"Professor Steed!" she called out. Spinning to greet her, a smile lit his handsome face. Grasping her outstretched forearm, he drew her close. She stopped short of a full embrace, aware of the eyes upon them.

"I missed you," he said, in a low voice so that only she could hear.

"I was busy. . ." She swung her free arm in the direction of Tasha and her Daniel. "A bouncing Miradon baby boy stole my time."

"Steed!" came the shout from his departing crew. An agony washed over his heart.

"When can I see you?" he blurted.

"I will come to you. Now go." She waved him off, the amber flecks in her eyes reflecting the coral sky as she watched him jog to catch up with his work crew. She sat where she was, her body tingling. She placed a hand on her knee to still the bouncing. *I am in love*, she realised. "Breathe," she said to herself as her other leg began to bounce a nervous rhythm.

Tony and Stefano bunched in the centre of the stone crew waiting to cross the wide stone bridge that spanned the sparkling river. Ever since they had volunteered to work with stone, Tony had been amazed by the precision and elegance of the houses and buildings in the village; a credit to the skills of the masons.

Years of engineering study had covered many areas of learning and a curiosity to unravel the secrets of construction. It had gifted Tony with an almost x-ray vision, mentally examining the structural innards involved in supporting the whole. The bridge they were crossing, now that the wagons had arrived, was a magnificent example: four arches with large keystones placed at the apexes, three legs submerged in the flowing water and solid anchors on both banks held the outer arches firm; an ancient and simple method, labour intensive, enduring.

Stefano ignored the bridge, his attention occupied with taking in the monstrous quark beast that pulled the wagon. The foreman of the crew, Gavinar, a tall blond of Scandinavian descent, had told them that the creatures were, overall, docile. Gavinar had explained that their diet was mostly vegetarian but that they had been seen to devour small rodents that scurried through their pen and in the wild, larger prey were not beyond their grasp, finishing by stating not to go too near to the head, just to be on the safe side. This had left Stefano with a feeling of trepidation and with more questions than answers that he feared knowing. Gavinar had chuckled at the sight of his paling face and had told him not to worry. The stone crew passed the lumberyard where more beasts and workers were visible through the stockpile of silver wood. Etherialists piloted a hovering train from the quarry. Large, exact cuboids of rock sat waiting to be loaded onto the quark-pulled wagons.

"Okay, men – get into your exo-harnesses. We got some rock to load!" shouted Gavinar.

Tony and Stefano helped each other into their harnesses. They were heavy and worn like a jacket, with strapping that supported the stomach, back, shoulders and chest. Tony slid his hands into the gauntlets and activated the harness. Pistons ran externally over the exo-jacket, connecting forearms to biceps and shoulders. Behind him, Stefano activated his suit, an excited look on his face, eager to put the robotic engineering to the test.

"Let's do this," he said, flexing his robotic muscles.

The hover-train carried several hundred blocks of stone of various sizes. Taking the lead from Gavinar, they set to work. The first blocks were loaded onto the wagon, the quark beast contentedly munching purple leaves from a nose bag. Tony laughed out loud at the sight of Stefano pressing above his head what had to be a two hundred-pound block of rock.

"These suits are amazing," he said, trying a one-handed balance that tipped him on his side, the fallen rock clattering against the wagon wheel, earning him a roar from the beast and an admonishment from Gavinar.

Sean Steed had finished in the woodyard. Some of his crew headed for the pub but he wanted to be alone or at least craved the company of just one person: Deb Sinclair. She was on his mind as he rounded the corner just past the bakery. His nostrils savoured the aromas, his belly acknowledging the scents with a low growl. He could not think of eating. On the other side of the pathway, a few doors ahead, hung a sign, beautifully carved from a solid piece of silver-wood. It read, Artisan. Stopping by the door, a female voice encouraged his curiosity.

"Come in. . ."

Sean entered the shop, wind chimes tinkling as his shoulder brushed past them. A young woman sat at a work-bench by the window, copper wire and a soldering gun lay amongst beads and coloured gemstones.

"My name is Marina." Her voice was like music, melodical. She was dressed in a skin-tight, copper-brown cloth, synched round her slender waist by a belt of turquoise beads. She was braless and Steed averted his eyes from her nipples. Too late.

"Sean Steed," he said, focusing on her face.

Marina shook his bionic hand with a smile. "See anything you like?" She asked.

"I like your belt," he recovered, pointing at her hips.

"I have several. Here – let me show you." She moved past him. Both her arms were tattooed: stars and moons hung between geometric designs. Her hair, he noticed, was dreaded with long braids of different colours, like autumn, he thought.

"These are beautiful," he said, holding the five different belts, crafted with care. "You craft everything in here, Marianna?"

"Marina," she corrected. "Like a harbour. I often provide shelter, and yes everything you see, I have created."

"What is in these small pots?" asked Steed, eyeing a collection, stacked on a trestle like cupcakes at a tea-party.

"Those are cosmetics: natural, of course. My shade is made from the purple-leafed plant that the quark beasts eat," she purred, pouting her lips like she was blowing him a kiss. Spotting a shade very similar to Deb Sinclair's, his heart fluttered.

"Can I take this?" he asked, lifting the small pot of matt-red paste. "And this belt" he added, holding up a string of diamond-shaped leather patches, inlaid with azul and golden gemstones, looped together with a yellow wire.

"A fine choice, Sean Steed. The lipstick is made from dried poppy flowers and pomegranate bark, ground smooth and with a matt finish," her sweet voice singing the words. Delighted with the gifts for Deb, he panicked as he realised that he had nothing to barter.

"Don't worry," she said, reading his face. "These gifts are for you. In the future, I will ask something from you and you will give it."

Sean nodded. The deal felt strange. *But hey*, he thought, *everything feels strange.*

He left the shop. Marina, trilling her goodbyes, headed back toward her work-bench.

Small slabs of dried dung crackled in the fireplace, shadows flickering on the walls behind Kalianne Devarioux, her newly sharpened mabrial quill dipping regularly into the ink-pot.

Her calligraphy had greatly improved over the years since her mother had begun teaching her. Kalianne had developed her own style. Flowing and sweeping curls dried behind her hand with a natural fluidity to her motions, the pulp sheets readily absorbing the ink. Reading any of her documents left the reader in no doubt about the passion and care that Kalianne put into her work. Her joy was as evident as the words themselves.

Kalianne had moved into her own house shortly before her mother's death. She was only sixteen but possessed all the skills needed for a life on her own, her teenage streak of independence winning over her mother's protests. Her mother's house still lay empty. Kalianne tended the small garden as much to honour her childhood home as to admire the splashes of colour that she had added, placed so that she could see them; an extension of her own flower-beds.

Perhaps one of the newcomers could live here, she thought. *It would be nice to have some life in the house again.*

Dipping the quill and wiping the excess beetsap from the nib, she began another sinuous sentence, a meditative wash of rhythm guiding her hand.

Serge and Alexi had volunteered for a marble run, as it was furthest from the village and involved travelling there on the hover-train. The marble harvest had nothing to do with the planned construction of the new homes. The marble was a sellable product in which the etherialists dealt commercially. Marble, from the outside, looked like rock but when the harvesting machines laser-cut the blocks from the hillside, it revealed its beauty. Greys and whites with rivers of rose snaked through the blocks. A turning mechanism spun the block, pushing it against a buffer, polishing four sides to highlight the meandering patterns. Two end slices of the marble cuboids were left dull for handling and to give a comparison to aid the sale at the asking price. The etherialists were not big hagglers and nearly always got the price they set. The shift had been fun: the best part had been taking turns, on the return journey, at driving the hover-train; a magnetic repulsion system, similar in concept to the bullet trains on Earth. Approaching the sorting yard, situated behind the huge black pyramids of the docking stations, sent the twins into a now-familiar melancholy. The realisation that they were grounded was as depressing for these pilots as for any misbehaving teenager. It was flying that they missed.

AI 131 felt the charge flow up its forearm, the power trickle feeding the batteries. The etherialist that had been working on the incapacitated bots glided over to the end of the charge wall. A panel lit, emanating a green glow from the screen, the light mixing with the white face of this vaporous being. Raising an arm to the panel monitor, the light-cuffs activated. The AI bot team were held firm at the head, chest, hips, knees and feet by the light-cuffs. The charging continued.

Data drain and erase began, wiping storage, memory and all protocols. The buyer had asked for a 'clean slate', his own learning algorithms to be applied upon delivery, his only stipulation was to receive his bot purchases with full batteries.

Blandar was a planet famously frequented by the rich and famous, aliens in need of servants to cater to all their needs and tastes and tasks. These bots had fetched a worthy number of crystals.

AI 131 and the others could still feel the trickle of the charge, video and audio recordings simultaneously spun backwards, images strobing between black as the data was captured then erased; sounds in high speed, pulled from memory cells into silence. Binary algorithms cascaded by the millions, ones and zeros lessening before the first line of script unravelled to blank, dark, nothingness.

The cuffs puffed off, the charge indicators ascending to one hundred per cent. The packing boxes were wheeled through a door at the far end of the facility. The etherialist technicians worked on.

Chapter 12

Reverend Sinclair's dream body emerged from the dim light of the forest, flat ground extending before him, another tail of ridges and peaks curving in the distance. Following the flat expanse of the valley floor, Sinclair followed his intuition, his faith proving to be fruitful. The valley narrowed, hemmed in by steep rock cliffs on either side. Then he saw it, gleaming gold: the tall crucifix perched on top of the church, two or three times the size of the surrounding buildings, a revered edifice, a true place of worship. Confident in his steps, he surged forward. The inhabitants noticed his arrival and were gathering to greet him. His eye caught sight of the mabrial, soaring high over the community, gliding effortlessly on the updrafts from the canyon.

"Welcome," the voice said.

The etherialist stared at Sinclair as he struggled from his dream state back to his reality.

"You are feeling much better," the nurse informed him. "Soon you can join the community."

The insubstantial body wafted from the room. Ambition and purpose flooded Sinclair's mind; his dream had awoken his greed for power. The Almighty was guiding him. A chuckle escaped his throat as he lay back on his pillow.

The combined efforts of the villagers and the newcomers was proving incredibly productive: construction of the simple homes was proceeding at an astonishing rate. The village planner had made additions to previous plans and had extended the golden curve layout of the village, spiralling the pathways outwards, curling naturally to accommodate the new homes. Stone foundations sat upon quarried gravel. It had been decided that four homes could be built simultaneously, given the spread of numbers the allotted work crews provided. The temporary domes would provide shelter until the work was complete. Clay soil was being mixed with a fine sand and river water to be used as a mortar between the stone blocks, allowing the homes to breathe, as well as acting as a glue for the stonework. The precision of the cut of the individual stones made the laying of the walls easy; it was like building by numbers. The newcomers had randomly picked their domes and it was suggested, and acknowledged, that the inhabitants of the geodesic domes furthest from the auditorium would transfer into the first completed homes. Personal touches and customisations could be added once everyone was housed.

The rhythm of the moon cycles encouraged a natural night and day shift. Salask and empere acted as morning and afternoon, with the deeper, violet light provided by amythesia considered as the evenings. Scheduling was convivial: the ease of life and all combined activities smelled of pride, the aroma of contentment permeated the atmosphere of the expanding community.

Deb knocked on the door of Sean's dome, her heart beating in her ears, her breathing laboured. No answer. She knocked again, then turned the handle, peeking round the door. On the left, a dung fire burned in the hearth.
"Hello!" she enquired, stepping in and closing the door. Running water could be heard from the shower-room.

Sean Steed lathered soap on his body, the hot water, circulating through the built-in pipes connected to a vessel above and behind the fireplace, rinsed the shampoo from his hair and relaxed his shoulder muscles.

Deb stared at the lather running over his buttocks.

"Can I do your back?" she asked.

Sean whirled, surprised and delighted to see her. Deb pulled her tunic over her head and stood naked before him, allowing him to take all of her in with his eyes, her lithe body aching to be touched. Sean gazed at her hips, her breasts. . . Their eyes met and she rushed forward, lips colliding with grace, her right hand clutching at his left ass cheek, the water running in rivulets, suspended from the floor in the folds of their bodies, pressed together, fused by passion. She slid downward, her lips kissing the wet hairs of his chest, her belly then her breasts feeling his hardness rising with her descent. The fingers of her left hand circled his girth, a vein pulsed against her soft palm. Her right hand slid between his legs, cupping where thigh meets buttock, drawing her arm closer, her fingers caressed his balls, warm water trickling off her elbow.

Sean leant back, his shoulder blades finding the wall of the shower cabinet. Her mouth engulfed his cock head, her lips easing over veins until they kissed her own fingers holding him firm. Deb bobbed her head rhythmically, sucking his cock 'til it could swell with pumped blood no longer. Releasing him from her mouth, his cock twitched, swollen and beating in her fist, she stood. They kissed, their embrace strong, his hardness pulsing against her belly.

Deb turned, Sean's cock flicking over her right hip. She bent, stretching her arms for the taps, shower water pooling in the small of her back, looking over her shoulder, her sky-blue eyes giving him permission.

His bionic hand covered her taut bum cheek, its thumb opening her for entry. With his left hand he guided himself in, throbbing, his slow deep thrust met with her ecstatic gasp. They made love.

Curled up in the crook of his arm, the embers of the fire glowing, Deb felt a tear well from her eye-duct. She let it run off her cheek, relishing the joy. She squeezed his waist and gave silent thanks to the universe.

Sean leant forward and placed another slab on the fire.

"I have something for you," he said.

"What?" she said, delighted. He stood and went by his bed, picking up the tiny pot and bringing it to her.

"Lipstick. I hope you like the shade."

"Wow, Sean – it's perfect, thank you. I'm going to put some on." She rose, springing like a child towards the bathroom. Sean followed, wrapping his arms around her waist as she applied the paste. It really transformed her face, her mouth, full and bright, her smile shone back at him in the mirror.

"A little something else," he said, as he reached round her and cinched the belt over her hips.

"To go with your eyes and to make these tunics a little less frumpy. As for me, I really have to get some trousers made."

Laughing she hugged him close, the fire gently crackling behind the partition.

Standing together in the doorway, saying their goodbyes, Sean Steed and Deb Sinclair watched as two of the recon-mining ships rose into the violet of the moonlit sky.

The etherialists, having scavenged everything of value to them from the Space Station ships, were now returning them to Earth's solar system. The other mining ship was heading to a galaxy beyond the planets Pujoll and Massam, previously harvested by the etherialists for their silicates. This current expedition was purposed with mining lithium deposits.

The black ship that had brought the latest earthlings nudged the final jump-tower, propelling it towards the magnetic dent portal. The remote pilots on Miradon 2710 eased the point of the pyramid base through the gateway into Earth's solar system. The hull doors opened, releasing the AI pursuit craft into the path of the swirling asteroid belt. The Space Plane followed, ejected from the neighbouring bay, settling into orbit around the brown dwarf Beatrix 1, as the nose of the recon ship reversed universes, like a fish that had spat water droplets at its prey and then re-submerged itself into the depths of its own world. Returning to the jump-tower to be propelled on another reconnaissance mission.

Deb stood in the village orchard, her thoughts flitting between her husband, the wonder of the strange fruits hanging in front of her and Sean Steed; the memories of the passionate time they had shared. She was startled from her thoughts by the steamy spirit that appeared by her side. She recognized the etherialist's veil of blue from the birthing room.

"My name is Sharmish," it said, with a small bow.

"You helped with the birth," said Deborah, hoping her recognition was correct.

"Yes," Sharmish replied. "I would like to inform you that your midwifery skills are proficient." It smiled warmly, swaying slightly as if on the breeze.

"Thank you," Deb blushed. "You are very kind." She wondered if she could be of assistance, then remembered how absolute the beings had been in their proficiency.

"I would like to be so bold as to inform you of a matter," said Sharmish, a small smoke ring blowing from its mouth as it said 'bold'. Finding this cute and feeling a little more at ease, Deb replied, "Sure, tell me what it is you have to say, Sharmish."

"I could sense your pain; a grieving when you held baby Daniel, the pain of a mother who has lost her child." Deborah was stunned. Was this a trick? Questions queued to be answered. Sharmish continued, its arm extended, its delicate hand formless on her shoulder.

"Your daughter is here on Miradon. She grew up here; she is your blood."

Deb collapsed, a smoky hand catching her fall. "Absorb this news gently. Undoubtedly you will meet: your daughter is the village scribe."

Scanning Deborah's bio-rhythms and temperature, Sharmish ascertained that it could leave Mrs Sinclair to her musings and took its leave. Deb leant against the trunk of the strange figus, her sobs vibrating the huge leaves. Collecting her thoughts like a sack of stones, Deborah sought the shelter and comfort of her dome.

She wandered the outer pathways of the village, distant shouts and laughter blowing on the wind from the pub. Company was not what she needed right now. She had decisions to make.

Donny and Francis had different preoccupations, mugs of grale frothed on the table in front of them. Francis was engaged in competition with Jonathan Miles; the chess pieces, intricately carved, a gift to Tom from the outspoken artisan Marina, lay aside the board, again in Jonathan's favour. Francis was three losses down, buckling under Jonathan's cunning.

Martha had squeezed her rotund figure next to Donny, effectively pinning him in the corner, smudges of lime-coloured flour already evident on Donny's tunic, evidence of Martha's pawing.

Tom's pub had been built nearly five times the size of the homes, with room enough to accommodate the entire population. It acted as a second meeting place when the rains came. The rainy season was not expected for another twenty moon-sets but lasted at least thirty. This was a time when the temperature dropped and the open hearth of the pub welcomed the crowd to its flames. On the wall above the mantle hung the skull of a hill cat, the size of a basketball, the bone painted red, its rows of sharp teeth rendered in black, even its shadow cast upon the wall made the villagers glad of the sonic-field, the barrier that protected the valley. Ruby crystals burned from the eye-sockets, a finishing touch that Marina found comical in its intensity.

Kalianne had opened the windows of her home wide, the fresh breeze sweeping through the rooms, scents from flowers in the garden, where she sat, clinging to the materials and her bed linen. Kalianne stroked the white fur of her pet rattit. The creature had long ears, turning constantly like radar pans searching out noises. Its rat-like tail curled like a happy cat, grateful for the attention she showered upon him. She could feel the callus on her finger, a bump left by the quill, as she knuckled the soft fur behind his ears.

An instinctual feeling, close to dread, had cloaked the back of her mind and a change of air and space was her way of cleansing. She had a smudge, picked and dried from her sage bush which she would burn later, knowing that in times of doubt or change, clean energy was a good foundation for a fresh start. Perhaps it was the arrival of the newcomers: Kalianne could not yet pinpoint the cause of her feelings – a calm before the storm? She did not know but something was changing; nothing that she could foretell. She looked skyward, her favourite hue forming, a gift from the moon twins.

The rattit twitched nervously, a pebble bouncing off stone had startled it. Kalianne looked and saw a woman striding purposefully towards the etherialist complex. She realised, with surprise, that she could be looking at herself, the newcomer's hair flowing down her back, the same colour as the sky above. Kalianne calmed the rattit with a gentle caress. She noticed that she, herself, felt a mild irritation and cuddled the rattit close.

Deborah Sinclair marched, a determination in her step. Slightly breathless, she found herself at the window of her husband's hospital room. A smug grin, that she recognised, spread across his face. He waved her in.

"Aah, my darling Deborah – did you bring me grapes? He laughed, his voice too loud for the small space. Before she could answer, he held out his arms and demanded a hug. The obvious revulsion that crossed her face turned his gaze to anger. Breathing in and standing tall, she said it, straight out.

"I am leaving you Gerard. No – I have left you," she stated categorically. She watched as his neck reddened; his eyes, in an instant, grew a colder grey.

"That weasel Steed has sunk his claws into you, is that it? Well, we will see about that."

Surprised at his intuitive skills, Deborah was knocked off track before regaining her composure.

"Gerard, the village has welcomed us. It is an opportunity to start a new life, all of us–"

"You fucked him, didn't you," he interrupted.

The words burst from her. "Yes I did and I am glad I did. Look – all I am asking is for you to leave us in peace," she insisted, struggling to keep a reasonable tone in her voice.

"You two-timing bitch!" he bellowed. "I am going to string that fucker up!"

Her reaction and action was swift. Like a mountain lion, she sprang from the foot of the bed, landing in a crouch on his chest, spittle spraying from between her clenched teeth.

"You. . ." she seethed, her voice now a whisper, a fistful of his straggly hair clenched in her fingers. "You come anywhere near me or Sean Steed and I swear," she tugged at his hair, "I will cut your useless balls from their shrivelled sack. Don't ever talk to me again!" She jumped off sideways, releasing him. Turning at the end of the bed, she faced him, pointing her finger like a pistol at his pale face. "Stay the fuck away!"

The door swished closed behind her, the swiftness of her motion pulling some of the air from the room. Her jaw ached from the tension of the exchange, her fingers trembling with adrenaline. A small sense of satisfaction formed like steam rising from a kettle just before boiling point. She left the hospital.

Gerard Sinclair lay still, perspiration cooling on his temples, stunned by his normally timid wife's attack, stung by her words and their delivery, wounded by her adulterous behaviour. She had meant what she had said. Doubting that fact would be a danger.

Sinclair lay in the room, thinking long and hard: his wife, stolen from him, an AI Bot team pursuing him, his congregation dwindling. His wife had mentioned that the village offered an opportunity to start a new life.

"You can do this," he mumbled to himself. Thoughts stumbled through his mind. *I can turn this all around. I will win my wife back by leading the villagers to salvation. She will see me in all my glory. I will get the twins to fly us all off this godforsaken planet; maybe even trick the bots into taking us to Space Station 4 and eliminate them, once we are out of reach from these intangible no-bodies.* Chuckling at his own derogatory pun, his confidence building, he pulled on his tunic and his flight boots. Fashioning a dog-collar from a bookmark that he found on a shelf, he grinned at his own ingenuity.

"Now they will know who I am," he said out loud, adjusting his collar. Reverend Gerard Sinclair strode from the room.

"There is work to be done – God's work – and I am his messenger."

Chapter 13

The Reverend Sinclair walked briskly toward the village, the light fading from violet and brightening to orange with the rising of salask. He encountered four teenage boys, two of them wrestling inside a small stone circle, cheered on by the other two. He stopped and enquired as to where he might find the adults.

"I don't know; probably building," one of them shrugged, pointing further down the winding path. Sinclair hiked on, arriving at a set of new, stone foundation plots; a rectangle of blocks that had been laid three tiers high on a bed of gravel, the third tier peeking over the ground level of the excavation. Four men were working a clay-sand mixture in preparation for binding the next block layer. Sinclair, not recognising any of them, asked where the newcomers were.

"They will be coming," one said. "Are you here to help with the mortar mixing or the block work?"

"Neither. I am here to do God's work. I am the Reverend Sinclair." Puzzled grins appeared on the men's faces, holding back urges to laugh.

"Well, this is a building site. We're not much for religion around here. You can bless the site if you want to, but when the stone wagon arrives there will be work to be done." Emphasising 'building' and 'work' sent a clear message.

Moving on past the men, murmuring and shaking their heads, Sinclair tried not to show too much disdain for their lack of faith. A man with a thick, black beard, split with an amiable smile, approached, extending his hand in greeting as they met.

"Hello. My name is Martin Norrell. You must be Mr Sinclair. So glad you are feeling better."

"Reverend Sinclair and yes, thank you." Sinclair followed Martin's eyes, taking in his dog-collar as he dropped his hand.

"Have you found your temp home dome?" asked Martin.

"Eh, no – actually, I have no idea what you are talking about," replied Gerard.

"Then please allow me to show you. We can walk and talk on the way. Perhaps I can answer some of the questions you may have."

"Fine. Lead the way and do tell me, where will I find the church?"

Martin Norrell gauged his words carefully, opting for honesty being the best policy. "The village has no church. We do not practise religion here: we found that it conflicted with our dreams for our future harmony."

"What? Ridiculous, pagan heathenry!" belted Sinclair, trying his best to loom over Norell.

Unintimidated, Martin added, "That may well be the case and also your opinion, but living without religion has served our community well. Here we are – your shelter." He indicated the first in the row of geodesic domes. "Perhaps you can think of another way to be of service here: ask for guidance. Your private protestations are, of course, your own."

Martin bowed slightly to Gerard as the Reverend stormed through the doorway. The door closed loudly without a word.

Deb observed her ex-husband and Martin. She quickly moved to intercept Norrell upon his departure.

"Mr. Norrell!" she called, coming up behind him.

"Ah, Mrs. Sinclair, your husband has just arrived."

"Please, call me Deb. And that," she added, pointing to Sinclair's dome, "is my ex-husband. We have recently separated."

"I understand. How can I help you, Deb?"

Her eyes met his, her gratitude apparent. "Due to our recent separation and now our close proximity," she pointed once again towards the domes, "is it at all possible for me to move my dome further afield? I don't want to be of any trouble but please – I hope you can understand – I need some space." Her eyes supported her plea.

Finding himself wanting to help this beautiful woman and compassionate to her plight, he squeezed her arm. "I will do what I can. Allow me to think of a solution, and do not dwell on your troubles. I am sure you will find your way here, and please, you can call me Martin."

"Thank you, Martin. Thank you." The two separated, Deb feeling a little lighter and more welcomed.

Deb met Steed on his doorstep when he returned from his labours. She held bread and vegetables in her arms.

"Can I make you dinner?" she asked, her bright red lips curling to a smile.

"That would be great. Come in," he said, opening the door and following her inside. She placed the food on the table and closed the gap between them. Standing on her tip-toes, she kissed him on the lips.

"Why don't you wash and I will set the fire and put the soup on."

With the fire gaining momentum and the vegetables simmering on the stove, Deb lit some candles that she had found in the artisan shop. Sean entered the room.

"Well, what do you think?" his arms spread wide, his fore-fingers pointing to his knees.

"New trousers! Not bad, eh," he laughed. "These tunics, although super comfy, they did make me feel– well, a little bit Scottish, what with all that wind blowing between my legs."

They laughed, embraced and kissed, a little longer this time and with a little more tongue involved. Eventually she poured the soup and cut the bread while he stoked the fire. The soup tasted good, the talk was smooth. Deb put her spoon on the edge of the plate,

"Sean, I have left my husband. He is now my ex-husband."

Steed slurped his soup, feeling a bit like a homewrecker, then not; guilty, then not; sorry for Gerard, then not.

"Good," he said, and slurped another spoonful. Then, ripping a chunk of bread, he added, "I'm glad." The rest of the soup cooled in the bowls, eventually turning cold as they made love on the floor beside the table.

Alexi and Serge were not feeling as content as the rest of the newcomers. The teenage kids thought the cyborg twins were cool and pestered them to show them their optical orbs, and tested their heat-detection sensors with games of hide and seek. This was all wearing thin and the twins had fallen into a state of dejection and melancholy. Observing the two mining ships taking off only served as a reminder to them both of the unexplored universe that surrounded them and being unable to pilot through the wondrous galaxies above, leaving them both feeling a little useless and out of place. The hover-train and harvesting machines had been fun to operate, a quirky novelty, but novelties were what they remained. The blur of starlight at the controls of a Space Plane or a jump-jet was what stirred their passion.

Polishing dust from their wrap-around sunglasses, they decided to head over the river to the lumber yard, as yet unexplored, and to see what thrills, or not, could be sought out there. As they wound down the curving pathway towards the bridge, kicking pebbles to each other for mild entertainment, their game was interrupted by the sight of Gerard Sinclair ducking out of the doorway of the farthest dome in the row. The twins think-linked together, their orbs zooming in on the doctor. An eruption of laughter burst simultaneously from them, the doom and gloom of their temperament evaporating at the ridiculous and comical sight of the Reverend's homemade clerical collar. The same thoughts coinciding in unison: *What a delusional clown, but at least he is following his passion.* This latter thought cloaked the twins in the dark cloud of discontentment and depression once again. Alexi kicked a stone. It bounced off the bridge into the river below, He put his arm around his brother, determined to make the best of their situation.

Martin knocked on the silver wood of Kalianne's door. While he waited he admired the array of colour of the surrounding plant life. The door squeaked as it opened, a sign of the gathering humidity in the air.

"Hi, Martin. Come in. I'm just making tea."

Martin followed her into the stone cabin, still amazed by the differing layouts of the village homes, even though they followed the same generic foundation plan.

"Your home is lovely, Kalianne," he said, seating himself at the table beneath the window overlooking the garden and her mother's old house.

"Thank you very much. It is growing around me: half the garden has invited itself in," she laughed, pouring two mugs of chardrice tea.

"Good for your stomach," she said, handing him a mug.

"For flattening it or calming it?" he chuckled.

"For calming it. Laying off the grale might help flatten it," she mothered, "What brings you to my door? I thought you were busy organising construction crews."

"Well," he started, blowing steam from his tea, "there is a lady, a newcomer – she is in an uncomfortable position."

"Oh?" said Kalianne, intrigued.

"Yes, she has recently separated from her husband and wishes to extend the proximity between them," he explained, blowing more steam and slurping a sip.

"The etherialists could move her geo-dome," she suggested.

"Indeed, they could, but I had thought of your mother's old house. It is vacant and it would save us having to build another home. She has a new boyfriend, you see." His eyebrows and beard competed to highlight his expressions.

"I see," said Kalianne, her mind open to the idea. "Always the logistician, Martin," she added, unable to hold back the cheeky jibe.

"Of course, we would honour your decision either way but it would help her and also me, as I fear the rains may come early," he pressed.

"All right," she replied. "It just so happens that I was thinking the house could do with some life again. Tell them it will be lovely for me to have some neighbours," she paused, just long enough to see Martin's face light up. "But on one condition." She paused again, watching his face tense. "That they keep a handle on all the weeding." She laughed at the relief springing to his cheeks, amused at how easily she could toy with him.

"Thank you, Kali," he said. "I will let them know immediately."

"You are welcome." She poured a top-up into both mugs from the warm pot.

"I think you will get along famously; by looks alone, she could be your older sister. Quite striking, really." Kalianne knew immediately who he meant. A change was coming, she thought, mentally noting that she should burn that smudge stick.

Sinclair had been wandering around the village trying hard to find and recruit old and new members to his cause. The villagers, it seemed, were not interested in salvation and many of his old flock politely excused themselves, citing the necessity of work, building their new homes. When he had approached Isaac he was met with a defensive stare and a hard rebuttal to his persuasions. Finally, he cornered the twins.

"Alexi, Serge – so good to see you both again. Why are you not slaving away under the thumb of your new rulers, like the rest of the prisoners?" he questioned, manipulatively.

"Doctor– oops, Reverend Sinclair," jibed Alexi. "We heard you were recruiting again. How is that going for you? It doesn't appear that these sheep need a shepherd."

"Exactly, but a few – enough – will follow if we can offer them a way off this planet. We must escape this tyranny and you will pilot us off to a new life dedicated to faith and worship." Sinclair bounced from foot to foot with excitement, adding, "Steal our ship back from these overlords and fly us to freedom."

"Reverend, we like you – you make us laugh. But in case you hadn't noticed, the alien ships are gone, with our Space Plane we presume, and as you know, we have no control over the remaining ship that is still here, we are not piloting anything. Not to nirvana; not anywhere."

Sinclair's face fell as he glowered at the empty docking stations, the single pyramid left as if only to heighten his anxiety. Compassion rose in Serge witnessing Sinclair's plight.

"Good luck, Reverend. We have our own troubles to consider. See you around." Serge wanted to add an advisement about removing the dog-collar but reconsidered and held back, feeling that Sinclair was best left to his own devices, even if all it brought was ridicule. They departed feeling emotionally heavier for the encounter.

Sinclair, feeling more than disheartened at the realisation that the Space Plane was gone, decided to regroup and reconfigure his ideas back in the relative comfort of solitude in his dome. Head down, lost in thought, he was startled by Sean Steed exiting his shelter. Rage flooded behind his prominent forehead, his large hands balling into fists. Professor Steed stood, his body aware of the aggressive stance of his lover's ex-husband before him. The silent stand-off thickened the atmosphere surrounding both men. A bubble of intensity blocked out all vision beyond the focus of their stare. Sinclair could feel his jugular thumping against his dog-collar, distracting him from his thoughts of attack.

Steed's mind was blank, his focus awaiting any movement from the man before him. A shadow passed between them, immediately accompanied by a sharp shriek. The giant mabrial banked towards the river, gliding toward the hills. The momentary shift of focus proved to be enough to end the stalemate. Both men exhaled, then inhaled deeply. Sinclair spat on the ground between them and walked on without a word.

Sean Steed exhaled a long breath, flicked some dust with the side of his boot to cover the phlegm at his feet, relieved that the encounter hadn't come to a physical altercation. *I'm a lover and not a fighter, but that man might well change that,* he mused. A vision of Deb filled his head: his heart rate maintained its elevated rhythm by picturing her alluring beauty.

Deb found Sean in the pub. His head stooped over a mug of grale, he looked frazzled.

"Hi," she said, waving to Tom for a separg wine, mouthing the words as she slid in at the table, seating herself opposite her lover.

"Hi," he replied, brightening at the sight of her.

"You look a bit gloomy. What's up?" she asked.

"I bumped into Gerard earlier. It was pretty intense. Thought he was going to attack me, but he didn't, although he did get a few blows in with his eyes." Tom proudly presented Deb with her wine.

"Thanks, Tom." She turned her attention back to Sean, with a reassuring hand placed over his. "Forget him: I have some good news," she beamed. Looking up from his grale, he took in her face.

"Go on, then – don't keep me in suspense," he said, entranced, squeezing her proffered hand with his thumb.

"I saw Martin Norrell and he has found us a home; a vacant one, ready to move into." She paused. "Together, if you want to." Her eyes sparkled, giving voice to her plea, a sky-blue and gold song.

"I would love to. That is great news. When?"

"As soon as we'd like. He gave me the directions." she said, lifting her wine with her free hand. "Cheers – to new beginnings."

"Together. Cheers, beautiful woman." His salutations wiped all gloom from his mind.

"What do you say to another couple of drinks, then a romantic stroll passed the lumber yard," he smirked, "then we can lie in each other's arms in front of a roaring dung fire and talk politics."

"That's a great suggestion but let's keep the talk short. I have other plans for your mouth and it doesn't involve talking politics."

After his work shift, Sean met Deborah at the entrance to the auditorium. She reached out her hand to him, her long, red hair blowing across half her face with the breeze. He swept it behind her ear, a delicate action she hadn't expected from his bionic hand, still adjusting to its touch.

"You ready?" she asked.

He nodded. "Let's check this out," he said, stealing a peck on the cheek.

The gate to the garden in front of the house was ajar, held open by plants that had overgrown their borders, the pathway cracked in places where yet more biologicals had found a home. Squeezing his hand, Deb led the way in. The rooms smelled fresh enough, the cot lay bare, devoid of any bedclothes. Dusty slabs of dung were neatly stacked by the side of the fireplace. Deb swung open the window. Outside, one section of the garden fused with the neighbour's, the flowers a seamless splash of colour hiding the low wall. A single path meandered between short bushes towards a water well. Sean was preparing a fire to warm the room, having checked the simple lum for birds' nests. The taps spat some brownish water before running clear. The kitchen was small and simple, with four silver wood cupboards for storage. A sturdy table and two chairs bordered the kitchen window that overlooked the village auditorium and beyond to the peaks of the hills, the leaves colouring an orange band to the horizon. It was spectacular.

"This place is perfect, Deb," called Steed over his shoulder. "Let's walk down and get our bed linen while the fire warms the place."

They pulled the window shut as they left. On the way back, they stopped at the bakery, Martha bagging two small green loaves for them. Earlier, Deb had discovered the fishmonger and requested a single river fish. One of the teenage boys had caught it in the shadow of the bridge and had brought it up for gutting and filleting. Gordon, the fishmonger, had left the head one slice away from separating from the fillets.

"It is good for soup," he had said, handing her the hefty, leaf-wrapped package. Back in their new abode, with dinner preparations underway, there was a knock on the side door that gave access to the well. Deb opened the door. In front of her, like a reflection in a mirror, stood Kalianne. Both women stood transfixed until Sean's cough severed the connection. Kalianne, her arms laden with a basket, was first to speak.

"Hi. I am your neighbour, Kalianne. I have brought you a welcome gift," she said, indicating the basket of fruits with a nod of her head. Sean had joined Deborah at the door and squeezed past the stationary Deb.

"Hi, my name is Sean and this is Deborah." He reached to receive the basket. "Thank you so much. Please, please come in," he said.

"Perhaps another time. I just wanted to welcome you: this was my childhood home but it has been vacant since my mother passed. I hope that you can settle in and re-energise the place." She redirected her gaze back to Deborah. "I am pleased to meet you." She turned towards the well.

"Are you the village scribe?" blurted Deb.

Halting, Kalianne replied, "Yes, I am."

"Pleased to meet you, too."

Watching as the young woman navigated the small gap in the low wall separating the gardens, Sean Steed then shut the door, the fruit basket hanging from his bionic arm.

"What was that?" he said, referring to the strange effect the encounter had had upon Deborah. Still motionless, facing the closed door, her eyes vacant, her attention light-years away, Deb answered in a barely audible whisper.

"She. . ." she said, "is my daughter."

Chapter 14

Deb and Sean lay together in their cot, the soft-woven blankets covering them from the waist down. Sean was lying back, his arms behind his head, resting on the pillow, listening. Deb, propped up on her left elbow, her right arm resting lightly on Steed's belly, was explaining.

"I have never had to explain this to anyone, Sean; not in twenty-plus years. In 2029, when I was fourteen-years old, I was raped." She paused as memories of the event flooded back to her mind; the lamp, the pain, that face, caught in the light of the corridor. Sean shifted in the bed, his bionic hand touching the groove between her shoulder blades, returning her to the now. She continued. "I got pregnant from that rape and when I gave birth, to Kalianne," realising now that she had not named her own daughter, "she was taken by the state." She let her elbow straighten and laid her head on Sean's chest, her tears running over the bridge of her nose on to his warm skin. "I never saw her or even got to hold my baby." She sobbed, bubbles of snot gluing his chest hairs to her cheek. He held her tight, allowing her release, struck by the thought of how worlds, literally galaxies apart, they had met for the first time in twenty-two years.

"It is really obvious but how do you know for sure?" he asked. Rising and running to the bathroom, she left the question hanging in the air. Sean could hear running water and Deb blowing her nose.

"Sorry," she said, appearing in the doorway. She climbed back beneath the covers, her face cool from the fresh water. She sat up, trying to stop her nose from blocking, her crossed legs warming his hip. "We were chipped, by the state, for their records. When we were scanned, here, when we landed, the etherialists read my chip. They matched it with Kalianne's chip and they told me."

"Wow, small Universe," he said, trying out a smile.

"She doesn't know, Sean, I'm terrified." Her eyes drifted upward, lost in her mind. His bionic fingers found her hip and squeezed the soft flesh.

"You have to tell her, Deb. She has a right to know. It could all work out perfectly." His own words sounded hollow. The situation could, in fact, turn out far from perfect.

"She will have so many questions. I don't want to lie to her, but how can I tell her the truth – fuck." She sighed. She turned her head to look down upon him. "You are so handsome," she smiled, feeling grateful for his presence.

"We can work this out. Take things slowly. Let's get to know her and when the time is right. . ." he squeezed again. The amber flecks, floating in her blue eyes, flickered like distant stars. "This is a gift that, for now, can remain wrapped. You will know when to present it. Your heart will tell you when."

His words eased her pain, the turmoil lessened by his suggestion. Delaying any action was the easy way out, but for now she was willing to accept that. Unravelling the truths, hidden since she was a child, would take consideration, deep thinking and much wrangling with her emotions, *but with him supporting me, it's going to be a lot easier*, she thought.

"Thank you, Sean," she said, unfolding her legs and wrapping herself around him. Sean Steed lay in her comfortable embrace, unable to ask the questions that had formed in his head.

"You are welcome," he said, breathing in and filling his nostrils with the smell of her hair; a warm aroma, like hay.

Steed had woken early, showered, then finding Deborah still asleep, her copper-red hair splayed across the pillows, he had left without waking her. It was noticeably cooler this morning and he was glad of the extra warmth his trousers provided. At the northern end of the valley, amysthesia was setting, forming a violet cap between two peaks. Salask's orange glow preceded its emergence over the southern plains, eager to fill the sky behind him.

Sean had not slept well. Deb's revelations had stunned him, not only about Kalianne but about the way she was conceived. He had felt embarrassed to be male, then angry at the man who had shamed his gender. *What kind of monster would rape a fourteen-year-old girl?* he thought. The horrors she had endured were beyond his reckoning, the fresh facts instilling in him a determination to support and protect her with his love; a love he had thought he would never be able to feel again. He arrived at the lumber yard, waiting for his crew to arrive, watching the orange orb climb skyward, as he fed huge purple leaves to the quark beast through the fence.

Martin Norrell was very pleased, the joint efforts of the etherialists and the community of humans were producing great results. The roof beams had been measured and cut for the first four homes, their walls now ready for them. The beams for the remaining houses were milled and stacked, left long, in case of any unforeseen discrepancies in the block work.

"Just to be on the safe side," he had said to the lumber yard foreman, who was busying himself laying out boards to make the window frames.

"Right then, lads," Martin addressed the crew. "Let's get these beams loaded, the chuffanx is waiting." Some puzzled looks from the newcomers mixed with the knowing nods from the veterans. The quark-beasts hauled the loaded wagons over the bridge and skirted the outer ring of the expanding village. The first signs of the chuffanx, for the newcomers at least, were the massive droppings, burst, on the broad pathway leading to the new houses; great piles, steam rising from the dropped excretions in the cool air. The chuffanx trumpeted in salute at the approach of the quark beasts, raising its trunk high into the pink of the sky. It was twice the height of an Earth elephant, longer and skinnier in body, three, thick tails forked from its hind legs. Large flat swells terminated the tails, pressing on the ground for balance. Seven-toed feet, spread wide, formed starlight footprints in the clay surrounding the homes. High up on the neck of the creature sat an etherealist, the rose-pink sky showing, in patches, through its phantom-blue body, the fumes meandering in and out of existence. The chuffanx lowered its huge proboscis to the centre of the silver wood beam, curling through the gap left in the stacking. The etherialist's hands were placed on the back of the animal's head, perceiving the commands through a hazy touch. The chuffanx stepped backwards and turned, the beam swung into place, slotting precisely into the stonework. When the first wagon was empty, the framework of the roof was complete. All but two of the crew returned to the yard, some hitching a ride on the empty wagon, the others gazing back occasionally to take in the monstrous scale of the animal-crane at work.

Loading the wagon for the third house had taken a little longer: the quark-beast had refused to move past its food sack. It had taken two villagers and an armful of leaves to coax the beast the necessary few steps to allow loading. Luckily, the loading was completed and the beast sated enough by the time the crew had to make room for the next empty wagon in line. As the twin moons sped for the horizon, the last of the beams was slotted into place by the chuffanx.

Martin smiled at the sight of the roofing crew already making preparations for the first house. He reckoned another two moon cycles would see the four homes habitable and soon after the rest would arise, solid forms of their creative efforts.

Just in time, he thought, focusing on a small cloud forming in the sky below salask.

The temperature drop was not huge; just sufficient to notice. Mists hung over bodies of water. Veils were hugging low bushes and highlighting undulations on the plains like pools left by a retreating sea.

Alexi and Serge had volunteered for a shit job, literally. They were packing quark-beast shit into small wooden frames to supply the dung fires. With the rains expected in a few moon cycles, the village administrators had wanted to ensure an adequate surplus to accommodate the additional numbers who had joined the community. The brothers had volunteered, partly because hands were slow to go up when the request was announced but mostly because they had grown fond of the huge mammals. The beasts gave off a comforting air of contentment: eating seemed to bring them all the joy they needed and it went a long way to raising the brothers' spirits and sense of gratitude for the simple things in life. The twins took turns driving the buggy with the trailer, unloading the fresh patties, forming gapped stacks in the drying shed. It wasn't until they felt the tremor, rattling the ground in the pen, that they realised the smooth docking-bay covers were retreating, sliding open into their housings. Silently, the mining ship had returned and was hovering over the square hole that had rumbled open to receive the vast ship. Descending at walking pace, the enormous vessel locked into the dock sending small dust clouds into the air, the dull clunk of the subterranean locks clanging a sure-fast grip on the pyramidal hull. The twins think-linked their admiration at the precision of the piloting skills, patted the quark beast on its flank and rammed more shit into the silver wood frame.

Reverend Sinclair was having daydreams of his own. Asleep on his cot, his eyes flitting beneath his eyelids, he was delivering a sermon to his people. The church hall was packed up to the broad doors standing behind the pews. He could see his own large hands held aloft over the heads of his flock, eyes full of faith and admiration for the messenger. Amens and hallelujahs sang from their mouths, echoing off the stone walls of the hall.

He woke with a start, his heart racing. He reached for a tablet and slipped it between his smiling lips. A flash of two faces from his flock entered his head; a young couple who had impressed him with their devoutness. Donning his tunic and boots and adjusting his clerical collar, he left his geo-dome in search of Anna-Marie and Lucas.

Anna-Marie and Lucas had been introduced to the schooling programme on Earth by Gerard Sinclair, who benefitted from two of his most devout devotees accessing the space programme. They had both trained in the basics of quantum physics, and had grasped the concepts well. Their beliefs in faith were what had brought them together, eventually as husband and wife. Daily prayers were a way of life for this couple and they had been missing Reverend Sinclair's flamboyant sermons since the terrible event onboard SS2. They had been appalled to learn that the village had no place of worship and that the community, in fact, shunned all religious practise.

Francis was feeling a little down in the mouth: for the first time in four years, he and his best friend Donny were not going to be a working team. Francis had fallen back on his other friends, Tony and Stefano, for companionship and had joined the stone crew.

"Why the long face?" Stefano had teased, punching him on the shoulder as if to beat a smile onto his friend's face.

"Donny has succumbed to the advances of the baker," Francis explained.

"Hah! You are as green as her flour," laughed Tony, showing no sympathy for his friend's plight.

"Don't worry, these three little pigs will get these houses built," Tony said, adding his support with an affectionate stranglehold, his bicep squeezing on Francis's jugular.

"Wait 'til you see the exo-harnesses in action – they are so much fun!" exuded Stefano, with glee.

Donny had left his dome early, the effects of the grale from the night before evident from his sluggish movements. Martha had told him to be at the bakery before salask rose.

The job as baker's assistant had been offered and accepted over many mugs of grale and Donny was not sure that the offer still stood. He need not have doubted: the instigation of the drinking session and its excesses had all been Martha's, guiding the subject of her affections closer to her clutches like an angler fish flashing its bobble. By the third grale, Donny was positively running towards the light, with Martha pulling him into the cleft of her breasts, while Francis shook his forehead into his palms.

Martha was waiting at the door, sleeves rolled up above her chubby elbows, ready to initiate her apprentice into the ways of her passionate work. Donny quickened his pace when he saw her, his eyes turning from bleary to puppy-dog.

Martha nodded with approval at his punctuality, noting the orange glow of the moon's imminent arrival on the horizon. Reaching out a pudgy hand, she led him in, with an agility that surprised Donny, through the shop and into the inner-workings of her bakery. Appearing relatively small on the outside, the workshop in the rear was spacious, filled with machines, ancient and modern, juxtaposing eras, yet combining efficiency in line with production. Bulky, stone-wood ovens, loomed from the far end by the back door. Rows of modern mixing machines, piping gadgets, shining work tables and bread moulds lined the wall on his right. The left wall was centred around another sparkling work surface, with tall, lidded drums, holding a variety of flour mixes, standing on either side of the table. Martha pulled the lever on a metal door, the air smoking around her as the cool atmosphere escaped from the cold-room. She showed Donny laden shelves, pointing with a fat finger through the mist, naming ingredients.

"Okay, wash your hands. Let's get started," she said, pointing to the sink in the corner.

Lifting the half-moon lid on the drum, Martha scooped the lime-green flour onto the table, forming a hollow in the centre of the pile.

"Add some salt and mix," she explained, swirling her fingers round the outside of the pile. "Add some water," she poured a little into the divot, covering the pool with the outer peaks.

"How much water?" Donny asked, mesmerised by her powerful forearms.

Martha paused momentarily. "You will learn. This job is all about feel, Donny." She said, more with her eyes and her chest than with her words. "Now stoke the oven on the left with four sticks from the basket." Her nodding head bounced directions on top of her blubbery neck. "Then get back here quick for the fun part." She paused before adding, with an orgasmic expression, "The kneading. . ."

Donny was exhausted when he finished his first shift, learning Martha's tricks of the trade. Staggering wearily, and this time not from the grale, his body beginning to ache in places he didn't know could ache, he dragged himself in the direction of his geo-dome, the back of his tunic, the area covering his ass, coloured lime green with Martha's handprints. He fell face-first onto his bed, feeling slightly dazed and confused. With his face on the plump pillow, he smiled at the recollections of being manhandled by this walrus of a woman and his newly discovered knowledge of how to knead buns.

Chapter 15

The Russian brothers were taking a break: only two quark beasts were left in the pen, the other mammals were hauling wagons. Martin Norrell was making a final push with construction efforts. The twins had adopted an efficient series of steps in accomplishing the shitty task, perhaps too efficient as they would be running out of work soon. A break in the proceedings had seemed to make sense for both man and beast. The elevation of the pen afforded them spectacular views across the valley. Using their bionic eyes, the twins were zooming in on the forest carpet that clung to the foothills in the north.

"Perhaps this is a good time to interrupt you?" the wispy voice asked from behind them. The twins turned to find the blueish ghost of an etherealist, glimmering on the other side of the pen's fence cables.

"Commander Captain Merchantim would like to see you. Please follow me." The twins instantly think-linked and responded with a nod in affirmation. Closing the pen gate behind them, they followed their auroral guide to the flight centre.

Double doors swished open for them, allowing access to flight command. Their guide indicated they should wait. The commander had his dark, smoky back to them, hovering over a large monitor, his hands stroking images to life, then sweeping them aside. The guide whispered their arrival. With some speed, Captain Merchantim flew towards them.

"Gentlemen, I am delighted that you found the time to see me." His words came to them in their native Russian; even the dialect and accent perfect. Delighted at this, the twins said it was a pleasure, resorting to their mother tongue.

The commander continued. "Please let me show you around. I have a proposition for you both but first I would like to introduce to you my flight teams and my control hub." Merchantim ushered Alexi and Serge to his monitor. The monitoring station overlooked a large brightly lit room, rows of desks, several with holographic images projected from them, manned by etherialists.

"Here, below me," said Merchantim, pointing to ten driving seats built on metallic stanchions, "is where our remote piloting occurs." Two of the seats were occupied, the etherialist pilots reclining in the chairs, their arms inserted into steel sleeves, a ring of bright light surrounding the connection.

"The operational chairs are in mid-flight to a lithium investment. I have time before they arrive to explain my proposal," stated Merchantim, his Russian sublime. "We have been observing you, not prying or spying, but we thought it prudent to observe the integrations into the commune. Our conclusion is that you are not delighted by your new-found situation or your future prospects, am I correct?" He halted.

"Yes, you are correct," voiced the brothers simultaneously.

"Then I would like to propose that you work for us – as pilots." His words smoked from his near-black face.

"We are not remote pilots: sitting in a lounge chair holds no excitement for us. We are military trained fighter pilots," said Alexi, rather ungratefully, unable to hide his disappointment.

"We belong with a ship, bonded as one, linked to its passage through the cosmos," said Serge, hoping to sound less ungrateful.

"You have misjudged me but I have judged you well. Please allow me to elucidate," Merchantim whispered, stroking forth a camera image, fed from the bay of the recon-ship.

"This," he said, "is what we want you to fly and you will be glad to know it requires on-board pilots." Merchantim floated sideways, allowing the twins to step closer to view the image. Their reaction was even more celebratory than Merchantim had predicted. Jumping up and down, chest-bumping and high-fiving filled the next moments in time. The jubilation climaxed.

"When do we start?" they asked, stamping enthusiasm onto their acceptance.

"Let us go to the bay and see your ship close up. I shall explain the conditions and restrictions of your employment and detail the gravitational star-thrust system used to power your vehicle."

His azul eyes shone with a hint of pride and excitement. The commander floated ahead, Alexi and Serge skipping behind him like children embarking on a school trip.

"You will be prohibited from entering Earth's solar system," continued Merchantim. "Let me tell you, Earthlings are doomed. Very soon, humanity will destroy itself; the Mars colonies will, in all likelihood, be doomed to failure by the loss of Earth's civilisation, unless they accelerate an independence from Earth. Perhaps, when the coming collapse has wiped humanity from its planet, we can then look at lifting your prohibition. After all, Earth has several interesting resources to harvest. Do you understand this restriction?"

"We do," replied the boys.

Exiting the sloping tunnel into the mining ship, Alexi and Serge were reminded of the sheer enormity of these vessels, the huge pillars stretching above them, out of sight. Teams of etherialists were busy moving polished blocks of marble into the far end of the holding bay. Commander Merchantim paused by the door.

"I had a hand in the design of your ship. I personally would like to hear your feedback: it has been nearly two of your centuries since I piloted a star ship. I, too, had a passion for it." Merchantim's eyes flashed, a brilliance in the dim light of the bay. "Here we are," he said, as the door swished wide, his posturing indicating that the twins should take the lead.

The skin of the craft shimmered. It held the shape of a giant teardrop laid on its side. Like opaque glass, the outer hull barely reflected the lights dotted around the bay but seemed to give off a glow of its own. The top and bottom halves met seamlessly, like two plaice mating. The hull showed no doors or windows. Alexi reached out and touched the shimmering skin: he felt tiny dimples beneath his fingertips.

"The rough surface helps minimise resistance in some of the denser planetary atmospheres," said the commander, anticipating the question. Merchantim floated higher, his volume rising with his ascension, his hand coming to rest on the tapered end of the squashed droplet.

"This is the nose when travelling through liquids. The other end – the fat part," he chuckled, "is the front when traversing space." He lowered his light-body to hover at eye level with his new pilots.

"So how does it work?" asked Serge.

"The gravity generator produces a band of gravity at the front of the ship. As the craft gets pulled towards it, you get forward motion; the stronger the pull, the faster you go. Then the band folds in on itself, folding over the entire ship from front to back, then repelling the ship from the powerband, producing both a push system and a pull system in the same moment. A self-perpetuating stream of power fed by its own motion, the only outlays of energy are the initial start and then, as you can see here, the maintenance of the hover, gravitational neutrality. The speed is infinite: your only restriction is retaining hull integrity. Your training begins when your duties in the village draw to an end. Mr Norrell and his administrators would appreciate your help, at least until construction is complete. Any questions?"

They laughed. "Yes, we have questions – a lot of questions. How do we get inside is the first one."

"Let me show you," Merchantim said, fingering a small fob suspended in his translucent hand.

Jonathan Miles had noticed the Reverend Sinclair's attempts to lure people of faith. He had also noted the vicious rebuttals that the self-proclaimed man of vision had endured during his recent campaign.

"Reverend," he said, as he approached. Sinclair turned, happy with the man's use of his proper title.

"How can I help you?" said Gerard, taking in this stranger.

"Perhaps I can help you," replied Jonathan. "I have witnessed your attempts to lead the villagers down your path of religious worship and I can see that it is not going well for you."

Irritated, Sinclair barked, "And you have a solution, do you?" He adopted an indignant pose.

"Please, let me explain, then I can leave you to your business." Sinclair nodded his approval for Miles to continue. "Shortly after we arrived here, there was a split in the community. Several members who held religion close to their hearts left to form a village of their own, with the purpose of building a place of worship."

"And how did they fare?"

"We just don't know: we have never seen or heard of them again. They left, never to return. Our hope is that they succeeded and are living happily and flourishing as we are."

"I see," said Sinclair, pondering the possibilities and remembering his recent dreams.

Jonathan pointed towards the northern hills. "You see that deep cleft between those two peaks below salask? That is where they went. How far they travelled after that, we do not know. That is where the boundary ends. Their journey would have been dangerous: crossing over the line of sonic protection is not advised. Beyond the barrier is truly wild."

"Thank you for this information," said Gerard, his eyes focused on the distant peaks.

"You are welcome, Reverend. Good luck." Miles withdrew, heading down the winding pathway towards the pub.

Sinclair's powerful dreams had now become visions, guidance from above, signposts his ego could not ignore.

Sinclair, Anna-Marie and Lucas sat in the outer courtyard at the back of the pub. Tom had brought them a large clay jug of water and three empty grale mugs, their insides stained green by the frothy ale. Anna-Marie poured as the couple listened to the Reverend.

"My visions are guiding us, lighting the road. We must travel to our destinies. We must leave these heathens behind to wallow in their mire."

Lucas nodded shyly, looking to Anna-Marie for support.

"I have great faith in you, Reverend, and these powerful omens that you speak of only secure my belief in your honoured position as God's conduit, praise the Lord," she said, reaching to hold Lucas by his hand and also to stop his nervous fidgeting.

"There is talk of rains coming. I do not wish to wait them out. My offer of salvation to these pagans," Sinclair's mouth twisted with disgust, "has fallen on deaf ears. As soon as I have exhausted all possibilities and spoken with everyone who remains, then we three, and whomever else I can free, shall travel to our Lord's house and join our brothers and sisters in worship."

Lucas sat, trying to join with his wife's enthusiasm, his trepidation showing itself with a fluttering tick below his left eye.

Alexi and Serge had scraped the pen clean of dung, the quark beasts eyeing them from a thick patch of purple leaves in the corner.

The sight of their new craft, now hovering above the surface on the south side of the docking bays, had driven them into frenzied activity. Martin Norrell had been found at the construction site and the twins had begged him to be relieved of their duties. Martin granted their leave and wished them good luck with their training, having found out about their new job offer through Offimus.

The commanding captain greeted them as they burst into the control centre.

"I understand that you are now free to begin flight training," he said. The twins, barely able to control their excitement, were smiling broadly. "With your permission, we would like to insert two chips into your cerebral circuitry: one is a locator transponder, so that we can track you – removal of this will have its consequences. The other is a language chip with Etherialin and several other galactic tongues at your disposal, necessary for fluent communications with our clientele." Merchantim's phantom eyebrows undulated for permission.

"Not a problem at all, Commander. Insert at will," said Alexi.

After the chips were fitted and tested, the trio, now communicating in the speedy beeps and clicks of

Etherialin, approached the craft. Alexi thumbed the fob and the door emerged from the shimmery shell, sloping down to touch Miradon's clay surface.

The cockpit was high and centred mid-ship, a rotating tube, housing the seating and controls, self-adjusting to direction, pitch and rolls. Alexi and Serge assumed their life-long positions, each with mother and father symbolised on the back of their hands.

"Link with the computers and let's take a flight around the planet," said the commander. "And don't forget to close the door," he added quickly, seeing the twins already joining the flight systems.

The pilots engaged the generator, the colossal gravitational field now under the control of their fingertip movements. With no sensation of movement or momentum, the teardrop broke free from orbit, Miradon 2710, slowly rotating beneath them, passing the moons in turn. The twins marvelled once again at the stars pin-pricking the blackness of space. Ancient cosmic configurations spread colour across the dark canvas. Labyrinthine networks of gases and debris crystallising into nebulas, flowing around the craft as it approached light speed. The landing was flawless, the brothers spinning the ship through two hundred and seventy degrees, attaining gravitational neutrality over the exact same pebbles and clay from which they had lifted off moments before.

Thrilled and confident, the trio walked away from the ship. Alexi pressed the fob, lifting it over his shoulder without looking back, lost in the joy of flight. The commander led them to the machine bay.

"I am very pleased with the ship's performance. Your piloting skills will, I am sure, improve." A dark blue smile wavered from Merchantim's face as he teased the twins. Alexi, always quick to take offence, caught the smirk just in time. "This is your first consignment: the shipment is destined for the planet Blandar, one of our more prestigious clients," said the commander, pointing to a row of coffin-shaped boxes. The packing box nearest them was open, the lid not yet sealed. The Russians stepped over the open box to inspect their cargo. AI 131 stared blankly at nothing.

"This one, the owner knows, is free of charge, the damaged face plate is in lockdown, unable to self-heal. It is almost as if the bot wanted to keep the scar. The owner communicated with us that he does not mind this defect. The bot's future task parameters do not require it to be in public view. Report here at first moon rise for loading and by then your flight suits will be ready: they are blue, my favourite colour," the flight captain wisped to his new pilots.

The twins think-linked as Merchantim floated into the distance, unsure if it were the planet's lighter gravitational pull or sheer pleasure that put the spring in their step.

Chapter 16

Deborah Sinclair had thought long and hard throughout the last twenty-three years about how she could destroy the man who had taken her innocence. Some of the decisions she had taken made no sense, even to her. Driven by loathing, she had sacrificed most normal or conventional pathways of existence. There dwelled within her a compulsion not only to seek revenge for the atrocity that had deadened her spirit, but also to offer some kind of protection for all females.

Withdrawing into the cold, calculating darkness of her damaged psyche, she had entered into a battle with her own moral codes; those ethics, twisting and turning through the horror that she relived in her mind.

Deborah Devaroux' classmates would have said she was a bookworm, plunging into her studies with little room for fun, especially when it came to boys. Her teachers thought of her as academically accomplished but could not help noticing her stunted social skills. Deborah had extra-curricular studies of her own. She was a stalker; a secretive, patient stalker. The man who was the subject of her observations and cold intentions was the flamboyant preacher, the Reverend Gerard

Sinclair, soon to be lured and seduced into marriage by his rape victim.

Deborah had toyed with the idea of killing her rapist husband immediately. The old adage of 'keeping your enemies close' had sickened her when it came to activity in the marriage bed: she could not have prepared herself for the level of disgust and revulsion of that first night.

Her reaction had been to drug him, lacing his food and drinks daily, with Progestarine, a sterilisation drug that she had obtained in a black market deal, out of state. The high doses, in combination with the thiazides from his high blood pressure medication, had quickly rendered him sterile and impotent.

A small win for his victim. She struggled with letting this tiny victory be enough. The loss of his manly prowess had hurt him deeply, but his impotency meant that the female populace were at last safe from his controlling, power feedings.

Thoughts of murder kept her awake through long dark nights, stayed only by her childhood light, an inner brilliance, leaking from its crusted covering. That leakage had saved Gerard Sinclair's life, to date.

Deborah was now feeling the intensity of her motherly instinct, with the knowledge and presence of her daughter, Kalianne. Like a she-wolf, her hackles of protection were engaged.

The new-found love that Sean Steed had burst open in her was the opposite end of the scale from her passion for loathing. She had to get rid of Gerard Sinclair: one way or another, he had to go.

She understood, from her inner battles, that she was not capable of premeditated homicide. She could expose him: Kalianne was the proof. The implications would damage everything: her daughter, the village, her lover. Not for the first time in her extraordinary life, Deb Devaroux was stuck between a rock and an incredibly hard, hard place.

Sean Steed looked over his plate at Deborah.

"Deb – you okay?" She looked up from the food she was pushing around on the plate, unsure how to reply, knowing full well that she was not okay. Her silence was worrying Sean, but he understood her dilemma. Kalianne had been the topic of more than a few recent conversations between them. Obviously, Deb was concerned and torn about what approach to take.

"I am not so tired yet," his body acclimatising to the onslaught of physical activities. "Would you like to go for a vino down at Tom's?" Steed asked. Deb smiled, pleased that he was concerned for her, offering distractions but never pressuring or manipulating.

"That would be lovely – a vino, pre-dessert," she said.

Worried slightly, he said, "I didn't get a dessert." Pushing her half-full plate aside, she took his hand.

"You are my dessert," she said, batting her eyelids. "Okay, let's go."

Tom served their drinks with his usual cheer. Deb and Sean sat silently, staring at the flickering flames from their hearthside table.

"I don't think he has much chance of persuading anyone else. I would leave for the other village now, before the rains. I don't want to be stuck here: it's miserable enough." Anna-Marie's voice entered Deb's left ear.

"The Reverend knows what he's doing," said Lucas. "We will leave when he is ready. I'm okay with staying another thirty or forty moon-sets," he added.

"Well, I'm not," barked Anna-Marie. "A village full of the faithful – why wait?" she added, slurping water in frustration.

Deb turned to Sean, lifted her drink and swallowed it whole.

"Come on," she said. "It is time for dessert."

Sean gulped, but left half his grale sloshing in the mug as Deb dragged him from the pub. Her idea solidified on the quick march home, hardening into resolve as they energetically made love. Finally, Sean turned on his side, a snuffle snorted from him as he slipped into a deep and peaceful sleep.

Deb waited patiently, her strongest virtue, until she was sure Sean was fast asleep. She slipped from the bed, dressed and left, closing the door with the faintest click from the latch.

Sinclair's door flew open as did his eyes at the sudden intrusion. His wife stood before him, silhouetted in the doorway.

"Close the door," he said.

"No," she replied. "Get up – we are leaving now," she ordered.

"What?" Sinclair stumbled from his slumber, not understanding this turnaround.

"I am coming with you to the other village now! Before I change my mind." She looked over her shoulder, checking for movement in the village. They hurried from his geo-dome, the door swinging ajar with their rushed carelessness, rousing Anna-Marie and Lucas from their pre-bed prayers. The four bodies crossed the bridge and headed north towards the violet peaks.

"Reverend, why the rush?" panted Lucas, as they trotted to keep up with Sinclair's huge strides.

"God does not wait for the meek and the weary: our path is lit and we must follow it," said the Reverend over his shoulder.

"A storm is coming," said Deborah, bringing up the rear, sounding equally as evangelical, her tone adding a certainty to her statement.

The ground was less packed than on the village pathways; puffs of clay dust rose into the air as they marched at a furious pace. Anna-Marie was complaining about her aching legs as they reached the edge of the plains. Seeing the rise of the land before them, they stopped for a break. Lucas, the only one who had brought a waterskin, passed it around. The young couple sat on small boulders that lined the base of the mountain. Sinclair stood, surveying the valley between two jagged peaks, looking for a natural way through. Deborah wandered off to the side, looking for a place to pee. Squatting behind one of the larger boulders that had come to rest on the plains floor, the salty-sweet mix of her lovemaking met her nostrils, tugging at her open heart. Strangled by her decision, she could not turn back yet: she knew her husband better than anyone. She had to get him further towards his goal. His eagerness to proceed did not let her down as he called for movement to proceed just as she shook the last drops from a cherished memory.

The climb was slow and arduous. The gully that they were scaling was bare of the trees that covered the slopes on either side. Landslides from countless previous rainy seasons had stripped the gully of all trees; in sparse patches, low bushy vegetation stretched from between huge rocks that formed the boulder field.

The gully levelled off. Boulders from the cliffs, right and left, leading to the jagged peaks above, had come to rest around a tall, thick pole. They had reached the sonic barrier.

The gully dropped sharply onto the plains of the northside. Like an enormous lobster pincer, another set of ridges serpentined from the backside of the mountains, west of the village. Descending the northside boulders was more difficult than climbing: awkward leaps and precarious drops were exhausting them all. The orange promise from salask had been broken by their descent onto the plains cupped between the two mountain ranges. The deep violet remnants of light were all that remained from the already setting amysthesia. This was as dark as the planet ever got.

Finally, the foursome reached the flat of the plains, their water supply already getting dangerously low. The break was longer, the childlike questions of 'how far?' being answered with 'just over the hill'. Deborah's eyes told Sinclair to keep his distance and he did, still confused as to what had happened to bring his wife back to him, but choosing to focus on the journey that lay ahead.

The orange glow from the first moon had caught up and was creeping down the mountain that snaked across the plains before them. Stiffly, they began to cross, their muscles relaxing with the motion and the hydration the waterskin had provided.

Just over halfway across the flatland, Lucas halted, pointing and calling for Sinclair to stop.

"Look, by the treeline on the left." The group gathered together and looked down his pointed arm.

"What?" said Sinclair, "I don't see anything." Lucas dropped his arm.

"I saw something. Something moved, I swear it." He searched all eyes for confirmation.

"Another of God's creatures. It can mean us no harm, let's keep moving."

They moved on, Lucas craning his neck to the left. Deb felt it first, simultaneously on her forehead and the back of her hand – raindrops, the rains had come. She turned to mention it to Anna-Marie, and it was then that she saw it.

"Run!" she shouted. As if by command, the creature sprang into action from its crouching position by the treeline. It leaped to attack. Its feet were like gigantic tree frogs' feet, four gripping pads propelling it across the plain in giant bounds. It would be on them in moments. Like a radiator grill from the cars a century ago, the hill-cat's teeth led the charge. Sinclair had taken off at a full sprint, his long legs surging him forward.

The hill-cat sprang into the air, its retracted claws emerging from their sheathing in mid-air. Lucas felt his wife's hand violently tugged from his own. Deb heard his cry 'No!' reverberating around the mountain walls. The creature slapped Lucas, the left side of his head taking the blow, sending him cart-wheeling, while its hind legs pinned Anna-Marie to the clay.

Deb skidded to a halt. Reaching for a stone, she hurled it at the hairless cat. It bounced off its scaly body. The scream from Anna-Marie was cut short as her severed head rolled from her shoulders. The beast let out a roar towards the sky before sinking its teeth into the soft flesh of her side, tearing a tuft from her body like a golf club ripping a divot from the fairway. Deb turned to see Sinclair, still sprinting, his arms pumping like an Olympian. He was nearly at the first trees carpeting the mountainside.

The cat roared again, snapping its jaws at Lucas, who was hurling handfuls of dirt and pebbles and mouthfuls of anger at the monster ravaging his wife. Deb ran past the cat and barged into Lucas, pushing him towards the gully they had come from. The cat sank rows of knife-sharp teeth into Anna-Marie's lifeless arm, ripping it from the shoulder joint with a twist of its thick neck. Deb instinctively knew the cat would tire of its lifeless prey: they were going to be next. Lucas was hysterical, crying and swearing, spit foaming on his lips from screaming. Deb slapped his face, hard. He looked from the wild beast into her eyes.

"We need to leave her: she is dead. We need to save ourselves." Deb's words were solid: vowels of granite. The message sunk home. They backed away from the carnage, arm in arm, watching the cat slice into belly flesh with side-to-side shakes of its round head, its long tail towards them waving its counter movement at their retreat. Still backing away, Deb looked over her shoulder to see how far until they reached the base of the boulder field. *Oh my god*, she thought: the distance was too far. Lucas let out a whimper. Deb snapped her head back, facing the cat. As she had feared, it had lost interest in its lifeless mouse and was now, shoulders lurching like giant pistons, stalking towards them.

"Don't run, Lucas. If you run, it will attack." They backed up, the boulders drawing closer with each reverse step. Deb was right, the creature was waiting, moving at their speed, waiting for them to flee, then the chase would be on.

Deb checked behind her; they were nearly at the boulders. The cat looked back towards its shredded meal, then turned. Leaping into the air, it sprang back towards Anna-Marie, a warning roaring from its throat.

Deb and Lucas saw the other hill-cat bounding towards Anna-Marie's torn remains. Wordlessly, they turned and ran, jumping over the first row of rocks and scrambling upwards. For the first time since the attack, Deb noticed the spots of rain falling on the rocks. It was falling lightly, not making the bouldering any easier. The rain, strangely, felt good.

Nearing the top of the boulder field, they could see the sound beacon of the barrier above the horizon of rocks.

The two cats circled over Anna-Marie, clashing claws and exchanging hissing warnings, dragging and pawing at her bloodied limbs.

Sinclair had never looked back and was reaching the peak of the ridges opposite. Deb, Anna-Marie and Lucas were dead to him now. His only mission was to find the golden crucifix that stood above his flock.

Deb and Lucas stumbled under the invisible barrier; the black pyramids and block edifices of the ethereal base the only structures barely visible in the distance, through the rain. Descending to the floor of the muddy plains had been physical enough to keep Lucas focused. The boulders were slippery and dangerous when wet, drawing enough attention from his shell-shocked mind.

Deb's mind had been intent on getting them both safely to the relative ease of the flat surface. The slow, steady downpour had turned the plains into puddles and pools of mud, straining their already exhausted bodies. Lucas had gone into shock, Deb guiding him by the shoulder in silence.

Deb's mind blamed herself for Anna-Marie's death: it was her plan to lead her husband away from the village so abruptly. She felt guilty, she felt anger at Sinclair's cowardice. Lucas's grief was yet to pour over him, but it would. All these thoughts and her limbs more leaden, each splashing footfall heavier than the last. The shattered pair were near to crawling as the bridge came into view through the rains. Lucas slipped on the wet stone of the bridge, his boots slimed with mud, his mind fragmented, his heart broken. He stayed down. Deb slid towards the unknown pathways of her future.

Chapter 17

Deb woke, still groggy from the sedatives. Her unfocused eyes stopped on the translucent steam of Sharmish's light-body, hovering at the end of her hospital bed. Memories of the hill-cat attack pounced into her mind, her body sitting bolt upright. Sean Steed woke at her horrified gasp and lurched from his chair to her side.

"Where's Lucas? Anna-Marie? Oh Sean, it was awful." Sharmish gently pressed her shoulders back onto the fluffy pillow. Sean held her hand as she relaxed into the cushion.

"Deb, I– I can't believe you were out there. What were you thinking. . ?" Steed was frantic and had been since Deb had burst into the pub and alerted everyone there to the horrific events, before losing consciousness at the sight of a hill-cat skull hanging above the hearth.

The village community had flown into action. Deb and Lucas had been taken to the hospital for immediate treatment. Lucas had a cracked jawbone and had lost three teeth; the left side of his face, swollen. Offimus and two other etherialists had coordinated with Martin

Norrell and they had set off on a mission to recover Anna-Marie's body and search for Sinclair.

Deb clutched tighter to Sean's hand.

"I had to get him to leave, Sean. I was the only person who could hasten his decision. I didn't mean to get Anna–" Sobs of anguish drowned her explanation.

"It's okay, it's okay. . . It's not your fault," said Steed. Sharmish trickled more sedatives into her system.

The team assembled for a briefing on the northwest side of the bridge, pools of mud squirting between the paws of the quark-beasts as they waited for the directives from the etherialist riders, poised on their necks. Jonathan Miles volunteered to guide them as he had suspected Sinclair to have followed his suggestion. The rain was gathering strength, falling relentlessly from the thick cloud layer above. Lightning flashed over the peaks, the low rumble of thunder muted by the steady downpour.

The plan was that Civack would pilot the humans in the buggy, towing the hover-board behind it, and upon reaching the end of the plains, Offimus and Davimit would ride the gigantic, but nimble quark beasts over the rough terrain to where, from Deb's hysterical descriptions, they would expect to find– They were not sure what, if anything, they would find.

Civak urged the six-wheeled buggy towards the gully that split the tall peaks of the ridge. Martin, Jonathan and Francis held on as mud splashed from the rugged grip of the wheels. The quark-beasts matched their pace, galloping on the left and right, clear of the wake from the speeding buggy. The light-bar from the buggy illuminated each raindrop, and had begun to shine off the rocks at the base of the boulder field, skidding to a halt below the V-shape of the gully.

The quark-beasts did not slow, their powerful limbs propelling them up the steep, uneven slope with incredible grace. Offimus and Davimit crossed the sonic barrier, the beasts, leaping from boulder to boulder, downward onto the next plain.

Five giant birds hopped and squawked around the remains, with several more circling above. Offimus held aloft a pulse-baton. Sound waves rippled through the dripping atmosphere, crashing into the scavengers with an invisible force. Screeching their pain, ascending with audible flaps of their broad wings, they joined the circle above. Offimus and Davimit floated from the necks of the mammals. The skeleton shone pink in the bloodied pool; unscavenged flesh hung from ribs and hip bones. The hairy, eyeless skull lay next to a water-skin, some distance from the bony remains. A boot filled with flesh stood upright in the mud; Anna-Marie's shin bone, running with raindrops, was placed on the blanket. Davimit tied the covering around the last of the remains and secured it to the shell of the quark-beast. Sinclair was not in this valley.

The men at the buggy stared at the bag of bones. It was pointless to transfer it to the hover-board: it didn't even resemble a body. It was more like a small Santa-sack. Jonathan Miles enquired of Sinclair. Offimus shook his misty head and started back towards the village, raindrops passing through his body onto the quark-beast's neck.

The etherialists skirted the lumber yard on the way to the village cemetery, set at a respectful distance from the community. A hole had already been prepared in their absence. Neatly cut and bermed against the rainwater. Davimit placed the remains in the simple coffin. It was decided to proceed with the burial immediately. Martin Norrell would organise a proper ceremony after he had the opportunity to discuss the details with Lucas. The other sixteen graves in the cemetery all had the same marble headstones, polished and laser-carved with simple inscriptions. Offimus would see to the headstone for Anna-Marie in due course.

The recovery team, their terrible task completed, closed the gate in the graveyard fence with solemnity, the drizzling rain smoothing the burial mound behind them. Raindrops ran over the rippling veins of the marble that marked the village's dead, a row of glistening reminders.

Tom had removed the hill-cat skull from above the mantle and Marina was fashioning an artistic creation to fill the space. She had followed her intuition and begun carving a large, wooden mandala. Incredible detail was already emerging from the silver-wood sculpting, its intricacies flowing from her artisan fingers.

Kalianne had the miserable task of scribing the horrific history of Anna-Marie's demise. Looking out from her window, rivulets of rain crawling incessantly towards the sill, Kalianne saw Sean Steed and Deborah returning from the hospital. The woman definitely looked shaken, paler than her normal skin-tone usually reflected. The rains always dulled colours; the twin moons above, hazy globules through the clouds. Kalianne tried to refocus on her documentations but seeing Deborah had left her mind agitated. There was something about this woman that disturbed the gentile scribe.

All but two of the new homes were complete. Construction would continue after the rains. The temporary geo-domes would house the remainder of the newcomers, providing adequate comfort and shelter. Lucas had refused a formal ceremony and had asked to be left alone to mourn in his own fashion. Several villagers had delivered hot meals to his door, which he had accepted with gratitude, but no-one had been invited over the threshold.

Lucas knelt in the mud, his palms together in prayer, staring at the headstone inscribed with his wife's name – Anna-Marie Carr. Droplets spilled from the base of the letters Offimus himself had inscribed into the polished marble. Tears, mixed with raindrops, fell freely from Lucas's face. He shivered and stood, his shins sucking at the wet clay. He looked down at the flattening mound that covered his beloved wife, lost to him forever. No amount of prayer would bring her back to him. Sadness and grief clung to him like his rain-soaked tunic.

Sinclair scrambled up the steep, tree-lined slope, the undergrowth grabbing at and tearing his tunic. He was running on empty, thirst sapping his strength. His sprint to the base of the mountain had all but disabled his scrawny leg muscles and now the hillside was shredding his calves. The tall trees, their canopy blotting out what little light there was from the third moon, which battled with the clouds to shine on the soaking planet below. A branch snapped in the dimness of the forest to his right, sending a nervous tingle through his drained system and beading more moisture onto his damp skin. Fear was starting to get the better of his mind. The sheer size of the hill-cat had astonished him and the noises surrounding him in the forest told him that he was not alone.

Metre-long millipedes scurried over the dank rotting trunks of fallen trees, teased out of their holes by the dripping atmosphere, curling over each other's bodies like snakes in a pit.

He yanked his ankle from the grip of a vine that was attempting to wrap around him, its leafy tendrils yawning skyward, drinking in sustenance from the downpour. He could not stop: the living nature on this planet would simply absorb him. A mushroom-like turret pushed from the forest floor, blocking his intended path with its stretching girth. Stumbling to avoid it, Sinclair tripped and fell, his wrist snapping under his own weight, caught in the hollow of an upturned root-ball. He screamed with the pain, a sharpness shooting up his right arm. He pulled his arm free from the hole and laid it limp on his lap, a wave of nausea washing bile to the back of his throat.

Sinclair prised himself off the jumble of roots, leaning on his good left arm, and staggered upward towards a gap in the orange-brown canopy. The swing of his right arm, throbbing a dull ache, seemed to pool his blood around the fracture, swelling with agony. He would need to fashion some kind of splint, he thought, as he trudged through the undergrowth.

The trees thinned and he could see the nobbled horizon of the peak. The rain relentlessly poured down, its path now unbroken by the leaves. Standing on the crescent of the ridge, he gazed skyward, seeking God's guidance, his gaunt face lit in hazy violet by the third moon, amysthesia.

A pair of mabrial birds glided high over the trees, swooping in spirals, looking for prey. Another crack of a twig sounded below him, from where he had just ascended. He hoped he was not being hunted. He jumped down from the boulder he was standing on and immediately regretted the action, pain shooting up his broken arm. Shuffling downhill towards more darkened forest, it was then that his eye fell upon the trunk of a silver-wood tree, its bark damaged. A silver handprint was embossed in the rust-red bark. The mark of his dreams. Suddenly buoyed by the significance of finding this signpost from God, Sinclair searched for a pathway onward. Skidding down the slick trail, his boots slipping on the wet leaves, he stopped when he saw steam rising from a scat. Curled to a point, it was not thin, but it was certainly fresh. He scanned around for movement. Nothing. The trail showed no discernible footprints. Edging further downhill, his arm throbbed in the V of his tunic collar. To his right he could hear splashing, the sound of water on rock. He staggered closer to the noise. The cave: the water ran in streams between the boulders surrounding the mouth.

It was smaller than it had appeared in his dream and there was no roaring fire, nor would there be, but it was dry inside and God had guided him here. Exhausted, Sinclair propped himself against the back of the cave wall, laid his broken wrist over his thigh and watched the rainfall fill the oblong hole of his vision until sleep blinded him to darkness.

Chapter 18

Kalianne watched as Sean Steed left the cottage next door. Determined to get to the bottom of what was making her gut twist every time she saw Deborah Sinclair, Kalianne had come up with a plan to ask her neighbour about her recent, horrific experience, for the purpose of documenting the death of Anna-Marie from a first-hand witness view point. It was almost a cruel and gruesome idea but it was to be her opening gambit.

Collecting her tablet and breathing in courage, she walked down the garden path towards her childhood home, the plants by the wall ducking into their tubular holes as she passed. Tentatively, she knocked on the side-door. Deborah opened the door. She looked remarkably well, her shampooed hair pinned up in braids, her matt-red lips freshly painted. She wore a figure-hugging tunic, cinched at the waist with a beautiful belt, highlighting her hips, her bare feet having to wait until her boots dried out.

"Kalianne, hi. Come in." Deb stepped aside, allowing Kalianne to enter.

"I have tea made – would you like some?" Deb added, taking in all of her daughter's movements as she crossed the room.

"Yes, please. That would be lovely." Kalianne sat by the window. The room already had a different feel, different to the atmosphere of home when her mother was still alive.

"You have energised the house: it feels nice," Kalianne said to Deb as she reappeared with tea for two. Deb leaned on the table separating them,

"You brought your touchpad. Are you here officially?" asked Deb, feeling a little sadness creep inside her heart.

"Well, I had thought to ask you for an account of what happened. I didn't want to approach Lucas. Of course, I understand if you would rather not recount what must have been. . ." Kalianne could not finish her statement: it felt like a lie. She lowered her head to stare into her teacup. Raising her eyes to meet Deb's, she found her boldness.

"This may sound crazy, Deb, but ever since I first saw you I have had a strange feeling, I can't pinpoint what it is, I know we look very similar, we look like sisters, but I have a feeling I can't explain."

Kalianne felt a small weight lift from her as if she had been burdened by her unasked questions. Deb felt a peculiar pride for Kalianne as she visibly noted the tension released from the posture of the brave young woman in front of her.

"Before I married Gerard and became Deborah Sinclair, my name was Deb Devaroux."

Kalianne's face contorted slightly in confusion.

"Kalianne, I am your birth mother." Deb's words spun around the room in silence, directly opposing the noise inside Kalianne's mind. A cold wind of rejection and hurt blew through her heart.

"You left me. You gave me away," she said, grasping at the false gust of rejection, defensive in her effort to process the news.

"You were taken from me, Kalianne. I was fifteen-years old, unfit to be a mother," said Deb, reminding herself of her traumatic youth. Hearing Deb say 'mother' had momentarily flooded Kalianne's head with images of the woman who had raised her. Nearly half of the village community were orphans; the rest either Miradon-born or the original carers in charge of the orphans on board that fateful flight all those years ago. Kalianne had never felt motherless.

"And what of my father?" asked Kalianne, not really knowing where the question came from. It just arose out of her.

"He died," said Deb, the lie stinging her conscience.

"Did you love him?"

"Yes, we were sweethearts: silly, ignorant sweethearts, too young to know what we were doing. He was too young to die, he was killed driving his first car." Deb stated, amazed at how convincing she had sounded in voicing this impromptu lie.

Kalianne was struck by how amazingly small the universe had just become and by how so much was out of her control. A sense of letting go, going with the flow, of not pushing or pulling – simply being – came over her.

Deb sat opposite her, desperately trying to read her mind, anxious at being caught in her lies, her heart aching. Kalianne didn't understand, she couldn't, but she didn't have to. She filled her heart with love and compassion for the woman sitting at her mother's table.

Sean Steed entered through the front door, two small loaves tucked under his arm, rain dripping from the brim of his reed hat. A broad smile leapt across his face at the sight of the two women.

"Hi, ladies. Nice to see you, Kalianne," he said, flicking the door closed with his foot. Kalianne rose from her stool.

"I am just leaving," she said, gathering her touchpad. Sean looked down at her tools.

"Were you working?"

"No, Sean, I wasn't. I was just having tea with my mother."

The touch-tablet clattered onto the tabletop as the two women embraced. Swaying in their hug, mother and daughter touched hearts, open hearts, accepting the past as gone, beating together in the moment.

One of the small green loaves bounced with a thud on the floor. The women turned to see Sean scrambling to pick it up, an embarrassed look on his face at his clumsy disturbance.

"I like you, Sean Steed. Nice to see you, too," said Kalianne, dropping her mother's hand and picking up her tablet.

"Enjoy your bread," she called, opening the side door.

"Come for tea any time," cried Deb after her.

"I will," said Kalianne, watching the flowers hide in front of her and hearing them rise again behind her.

"Wow. . ." said Deb.

"You can say that again. Who would have thought? Finding your daughter, in a different solar system – what are the odds?" Steed shook his head.

"Wow. . ." she said again, wrapping her arms around his broad chest.

Sinclair felt two agonies, one right after the other. The first was a searing sting in his jugular; the second, the sharp snapping and grinding of broken bones. Sinclair's impulse to slap the biter off his neck had propelled his broken wrist from sleep to slap: in one agonising moment, he was awake. He was sure that he had further damaged his arm. The pain was excruciating, relentless like the rain outside.

The pinky-orange sky of the two moons illuminated the cave entrance. Sinclair could feel his top lip sticking to his teeth: he needed water. Rivulets ran clear and cold over the boulders. Cupping his hands under the stream, Sinclair slapped the water into his thirsty mouth, again and again until he was panting. The cascade falling fast enough for the microbial life to pass unseen.

His belly now swollen with cloud drops, he turned his attention to his arm. Discoloured and disproportionate, *it looks as if it doesn't even belong to me*, he thought. The roots that he pulled from the undergrowth were flexible and long enough to encase the splint sticks, tying them off around his bicep, the final knots with his good hand and teeth.

The hunger pains had subsided with the onslaught of water, but as his thirst diminished, the itch on his neck was becoming unbearable: the bite was becoming hot to the touch and was swelling, tightening his gooseneck throat.

With a hesitant step forward, Sinclair left his shelter, putting all his faith in finding the golden crucifix that towered over his future. Rain drops grew in the orange leaves above his head before gravity pulled them groundward or onto the shoulders of his damp tunic. The root-wrapped splint eased the sharpness of the pain from his snapped wrist bones but the swelling had replaced the sharp pain with a dull throbbing.

His boots struck the flat ground of the next valley floor settled between another ripple of ridges in the distance. Sinclair followed the treeline on the northside of the range he had just descended. He did not want to expose himself to the open plain and the keen eyes of the wildlife. Unavoidable puddles and pools of rainwater soaked into his wet boots, his feet squelching with every sodden step.

Sinclair heard the screech behind him to his left, fear turning his body quickly. The screech heralded the diving descent of the mabrial. Sinclair watched as the bird, following the steep incline of the tree tops, tucked its wings into a dive. The speed was astonishing: with the slightest of adjustments the bird flew parallel to the valley floor. Flapping twice, its huge wingspan maintained speed and elevation above the plain. The mabrial screeched again, raising its head and spreading its wings to land in its nest, jutting from the cliffside of the canyon where both ridges met.

Salask had already set behind the treeline and empere would soon follow the orange glow of its path.

One step after another, Sinclair sloshed towards the canyon. Weathered sticks stuck out from the ledge high above him. Rain dripped from the beak of his overseer.

The trees were giving way to the steeper, rocky slopes of the canyon. The pools were starting to form small streams, rushing to become a river. His way ahead was blocked by the vertical rock on his right, the torrent of water to his left, carving clay from beneath boulders, deepening the riverbed.

The shadow of the mabrial swept over the river as it flew deeper into the darkening gorge. Sinclair stood knee deep, looking for a way to proceed, his options narrowing by the moment. Water was streaming all around him. He could feel the strength of the pull, the gorge draining the run-off from the surrounding hills. Boulders disappeared, submerged by the torrent. Sinclair lost his balance trying to step to his left, looking for a way back. The water swirled around his thighs, tipping him into the current. On his back, the toes of his boots bobbing in front of him, his body was carried into the rapids. His hip smashed into a submerged rock, jarring his body and spinning him shoulder-first downstream. He fought desperately to fold his long legs beneath him and to turn once more feet-first into the churning rapids. He felt the water deepen beneath him, the gorge dropping from the steep sides, funnelling the raging waters through the V of the canyon.

The river turned sharply left, waves crashing against the cliffside on his right, riding the wall, eroding and scouring before flipping back into the flow. Ahead the river twisted to the right. Sinclair fought to remain in the central channel away from the walls, where the water accelerated over the stone. His broken wrist sent waves of pain up his arm with the swirling motion of the eddies circumnavigating the underwater boulders.

The cliffs ahead widened with the rushing water at their base, then narrowed above until nearly touching, before curving wider again like a massive keyhole. The water beneath the keyhole was smooth on the horizon;

no churning or swirling, only smooth grooves to the flat edge.

Sinclair realised the waterfall too late to save himself, but just in time to register the dread and terror that the sight emblazoned across his mind. His feet went over first, his eyes bulged then snapped closed, tight. His lungs sucked in a breath as the force of the water behind him became a rolling collar then a liquid hood, dropping his body into the vertical chute.

Lucas had lain in his cot, barely able to rise and stoke the fire with another dung-brick. His jaw was healing well: the nanobot injection he had received from the etherialist doctor was doing its job. Grief had swallowed him whole and then spat him back out into a world of anger and blame. He blamed God for allowing it to happen, he blamed himself and the Reverend Sinclair. He prayed, clinging to his faith. God works in mysterious ways, he had reminded himself.

It was the cries of baby Daniel next door in the neighbouring geo-dome that pulled him back to his reality. Tasha and her Daniels had made the best of a crazy situation, bringing up a newborn in a cradle of love, no matter the circumstance.

Lucas was struck and inspired by the simple act of caring and giving. The villagers had been supportive and respectful. Lucas felt that it was time to give back, to pull himself together and open himself to new beginnings. He would start with the new life form next door. Rising from his cot he went to the shower room. Looking in the mirror, he said goodbye to the old Lucas, shaved, showered, then wiping the moisture from the mirror, said hello to a new Lucas Carr.

Tasha answered the knock on the dome door.

"Lucas, hi – are you ok?"

"Hello, Tasha – yes, I feel much better now, thank you." Daniel Junior let out a disturbed cry, letting his parents know that he was in need of something. Tasha's face sagged slightly, mentally eliminating options.

"Tasha, I would like to babysit Daniel Junior so that you and his father can enjoy some time together," offered Lucas. Tasha was surprised and delighted, asking Lucas to come in.

Daniel Senior was hunched over baby Daniel, his son's legs pumping in the air as if he were on an invisible bicycle, while his father folded on a clean cloth diaper.

"Can I pick him up?" Lucas asked, Daniel Senior's work now complete. Daniel stood with his happy son and handed him over. Lucas's face lit up at the sight of this newborn cradled in the crook of his arm. Daniel Junior stared up at Lucas, his big brown eyes sparkling. The baby's whole body shuddered, his arms and legs stretching, before relaxing into limp contentment. Small baby noises passed from between his lips, swollen from suckling. Lucas was in heaven, his focus centred on this happy being.

"You guys are getting along," laughed Tasha. "Looks like we have a babysitter," she smiled at the happy pair.

Lucas rocked Daniel Junior on his lap until it was time for a feeding, his mother more desperate to relieve the pressure on her breasts than the baby's hunger called for. Lucas left, assuring the young parents that he would be available any time they needed a break from the pressures of parenthood. He walked down to the turbid river and sat on the now smaller bank.

The river of life, he thought, as he watched the heavy flow pass by. Picking up a stick of silver wood, he began to whittle what was to be a horse for Daniel Junior. Soft rain fell, not disturbing his focus.

Chapter 19

Sinclair's coughing and spluttering sounded distant in his mind. Water dribbled from his slack mouth as the agonies of his battered body wept into consciousness. He squeezed his eyes in agony before opening them fully. A cold, still pool, rippled only with the circular splashings of the rain drops, supported his dangling legs, his ribcage creaking under the weight of his torso hanging over the boulder. With a monumental effort of will, he spun his body into a seated position, his heavy boots submerged in the cool pool. The splint on his arm had been smashed in the fall, dangling in bits from the knotted roots still fastened above his elbow. His hip was badly bruised. He surveyed the area beyond the dark pool. To his left, he could see the waterfall, a coffee-and-milk-coloured mass, plunging from the mountains into the gorge.

By God's grace. . . he thought, wondering how he had survived such a dramatic drop. His eyes followed the cliffs down and across the pool: the river ran faster opposite, dropping again over a second set of smaller falls before winding and slowing in the broad basin of the canyon. Leaning back, steep rock cliffs towered above him. Tilting his neck made his throat throb, the bulge under his ear now the size of his fist.

Sinclair slid off the rock, his feet finding the bottom as the water reached chest high. He waded cautiously towards a boulder at the side of the second waterfall. Through the top of the keyhole formation on the cliffs, Sinclair watched as the huge mabrial stood up in its nest, extended its fuchsia plumage until reaching full wingspan, flapped a silent beat in the damp air, then folding its wings back onto its feathered body and sank back into its construction, disappearing from sight. Its ominous beak clacked out of earshot.

A thick, black snake slithered across the surface of the pool, longer than Sinclair was tall, the waters pulling it towards the falls. The snake's head lifted, its long body being carried over the drop before the stationary head snapped downwards following its tail. Sinclair watched as it resurfaced, its forked tongue flicking at the air as it turned towards the calming waters ahead.

From above the waterfall, Sinclair had a good view of the other side. With unscalable cliffs behind him, the relative flat of the other side looked negotiable. The only way to get there was over the waterfall. Drawing courage from the snake's success, Sinclair edged his way to where the falls dropped. His blackened hip complained as he crouched, trying psychologically to diminish the height. The water carried him over, its weight pinning him under until its force pushed him forward into the overspill calm and eventually the surface.

Clawing at the water one-handed, the shattered splint floating behind him, he swam and floundered to the far side. Dragging himself from the cold water, he lay shivering in the mud.

Across the river the cliffs glowed pink, extending downstream for as far as he could see. The small meadow, dotted with trees to which he had swum, ended at the river. It was a hill of trees, slowly being eroded by the touch of the waters. *If there are trees, there are sticks*, he thought, looking at the roots of his splint. *I must make a new one*.

He walked on, favouring his good leg from his stiff hip. The dead branches snapped easily to a good length, the roots holding them in place over his blackened wrist. Moving it from its unnatural angle back to straight had spun stars into his vision. Gasping for breath, Sinclair rested against the rust-red bark. The thin copse of trees revealed the violet-pink gap of a clearing ahead. Unable to stand, he rested, his belly grumbling with hunger. When he realised the pink was gone from the dim light of the sky, another surge of determination drove him to his feet.

He leaned on the last tree trunk in the narrow wood, looking across the clearing. At the river end stood some small buildings. Further inland, backed onto a thicker spike of forest, stood a large building. Leaning at an angle across a crumbling wall was a great golden crucifix.

Sinclair hobbled across the small meadow, tall plants sprouting from the damp land. The trees behind the commune buildings were blackened, charred from a fire, possibly a lightning strike. The church was roofless, beams poking over the crumbling walls that had once supported them.

"Hello!" cried Sinclair, his voice echoing off the sheer cliffs that held in the river.

Enduring the pain of his movements, Sinclair climbed the stone steps to the church door. One of the two, large, wooden doors lay on the floor within the church, the other hung precariously from a single hinge. Plant life filled the spaces between the pews and the roof beams that pinned them to their position of decay. The great cross had fallen to its right and lay on top of what had once been the frame of a stained-glass window. Although there was no coloured glass to be found amongst the dirt and debris, the vegetation was too thick. Nature was gradually pulling this ruin back from its styled structure and turning it into organics and rubble.

"Hello!" he shouted in desperation in the direction of the small dwellings. Panic was starting to take hold of his fragile mind, hunger and painful exhaustion tearing down his energy reserves. Nearly faint with his efforts, he stumbled down the church steps towards the burnt-out dwellings. Searching each house only cemented the conclusion that no one was here.

Perhaps they moved on, he thought, immediately rejecting the idea. Leaning into a door, Sinclair pushed against the obstruction. Light poured in with the rain where half the roof was missing, illuminating a skeleton. The beard from the dead man draped over the upper vertebrae and sternum, falling between the ribs. The dead man's bed was in the corner, the matting rotting.

With tears streaming down his face, Sinclair stepped around the corpse's bony remains and sat on the bed. It held his weight, complaining with loud creaks from the wooden joints. One-handed, he took his boots off, white flesh hung from two of his wet toes. Scratching the itchy ball on his neck, blood seeped under his fingernails, like litmus paper drawing up fluid, the lump feverishly hot.

Devastated and exhausted, Sinclair lay down, the bed reacting noisily. The rain fell steadily through the open roof in the opposite corner, its melodic sound tugging Sinclair into unconsciousness.

Chapter 20

Sinclair sucked in a gasping breath like a man resuscitated from drowning. He had no idea where he was. The dim light was soaked with rain, his body immobile. Memories flooded back into his head: the golden crucifix, toppled and flaking; the bearded skeleton. Sinclair turned his head – there, by the door, lay the hairy ribcage. His hearing picked up a popping noise, the faintest sound but it was close: a *pop* like a kid bursting bubble gum. The intense pressure on his throat abated, he placed his hand on the lump: it felt as though he had stuck his hand in a bucket of maggots. Pulling back, he stared at his hand – tiny, soft-shelled crustaceans crawled all over his palm, running between his fingers. He flicked his wrist to rid himself of these creatures.

Then, between his thumb and forefinger, he felt the first bite: a chunk of skin flayed from the thumb knuckle, then another, then another. A grey-black stream of shells poured from his neck. He fell from the bed, bleeding from a hundred tiny lacerations. Swarming from his throat, they scuttled under his stick-splint, tearing chunks of flesh from his forearm.

He writhed on the floor, screaming as they covered his body, the steady procession pouring from his neck, eating his face and filling his ear, piercing his eardrum.

Sinclair's spine arched in agony. Seconds later, flattened by a sudden weight, his torso was pinned to the floor. Sinclair's eyes bulged in terror. The giant mabrial, its talons sunk deep into his chest, hooked around his collarbones. The bird screeched then darted its beak downwards.

A sucking noise then a snap sounded in Sinclair's head as his eyeball was plucked from its socket. His other eye watched as the powerful beak sliced his steel-grey iris in half and with a flick of its head, tossed back his eye, its optic nerve trailing into its feathered gullet.

The cliffs vibrated with the percussion of his screams, then finally resonated with the bloody gurgle of the Reverend Gerard Sinclair's death rattle.

Chapter 21

After twenty-three moon-cycles, the rain ceased, the thrumming of the drops replaced by the tinkling of the last drips falling from the roof tiles. Some of the highest peaks in the distance had been kissed with snow, now reflecting the pink of the afternoon's moonlight. The air smelled fresh and clean. The pathways that ran through the village had been washed clear of the dust layer that had accumulated since the last rainy season, the stones glinting with mineral deposits.

The river still ran high and brown with the waters seeping from the hills, the fish hidden deep in its flow.

The whole community had jumped into action as soon as empere had joined salask in the sky.

Martha had announced her engagement to Donny during the rains and told everyone that the day the rains ended would be the day they were married. Preparations had been underway for several moons: every one enjoyed a good wedding. It had been a long time since the last one and an excitement ran palpably throughout the community.

It was to be a simple humanist ceremony and Martin Norrell was to conduct the proceedings. The best man, Francis, was busy trying to steady the groom's nerves, mostly by laughing at him and poking fun at Donny's obvious anxiety. A small bottle of Tom's secret moonshine passed between them.

The auditorium was alive with lighting crews, decorators and villagers filing up and down the steps with catering supplies and bunting. Martha was constructing and putting the finishing touches onto her own massive wedding cake, her avatar using most of the wax ball Marina was working on.

Kalianne would be recording the ceremony but for now she was gathering a bouquet with her mother in the garden. A shadow momentarily blocked the moonlight as a mabrial bird circled low over the cottages.

"Look!" squealed Kalianne, pointing skyward to a long orange tail feather swinging in arcs towards the ground. The bird landed briefly next to the low wall separating the gardens. The tail feather came to rest on the lid of the well. Kalianne ran excitedly to collect it. The bird flapped its huge wings and Deb saw something fall from its beak. The mabrial rose into the sky with powerful strokes before gliding over the river towards the hills. Deb went to see what the bird had dropped. Nestled under the branches of the beatsap bush lay a ringed finger, the gold band stuck between a frill of severed flesh and the knuckle. The fingernail was black and bloody, a section of bone showing between both knuckles.

Deb prized the ring over the ridge of flesh, quickly pressing the finger deep into the soil between the roots of the bush, before looking for the inscription. She had just read 'G from D', when Kalianne's voice sounded behind her.

"What have you got there?" she asked. Deb spun round, standing up, and held out her hand.

"Here, for you." She said. "For your new quill." Kalianne took the branch, laden with a cluster of beatsap berries, from her hand.

"Thanks, Mum. Gifts from the universe," she exclaimed happily, holding up the berries and the tail feather. Deb felt the ring drop deeper down inside her boot.

"Let's finish this bouquet and then I can help you prepare some fresh ink," said Deb, her mind calming, her body softening and her heart opening. *Gifts and blessings from the universe, indeed,* she thought, watching her daughter's hair blend perfectly with the sky.

The Space Plane had appeared on the monitors of SS4's control centre three minutes and thirty-three seconds after they had lost contact. The rescue team had reported back that the AI Bot craft was smashed to bits, fragments found swirling in the asteroid belt surrounding the brown dwarf Beatrix 1. A panel with the space project logo and the identification numbers had been recovered from the stream of the belt as proof for the commanders. The rest of the torn shards were left spinning in the current of the asteroid swirl.

All lifeforms from the jump plane were lost, presumed dead. The mystery of the disappearance of the passengers and crew, the propulsion and flight systems, stripped from the hollow hull and the smooth, vacuous space where once the magnetic dent had been, kept the media and scientists alike positing and puzzling over theories for years to come.

Donny and Francis stood in the centre of the auditorium. Donny was now having to steady his best friend and best man as the effects of Tom's grog circulated through Francis's system. Donny's nerves steady, the pair waited for the arrival of the bride.

Amysthesia was rising from the south as empere pulled its pink light behind the mountains to the north.

Murmurs went around the top of the amphitheatre as the highest rows of guest spectators caught sight of Martha, being led, arm-in-arm, by Gavinar onto the top step. She was resplendent in her silken robe, her hair tied high on her head and pinned with delicate flowers. She looked radiant. Donny nudged Francis in the ribs to save him from nodding off and Francis responded by pulling himself together and whipping out the rings to show Donny and Martin that he was taking his responsibilities seriously.

Offimus and several of the etherialists hovered at regimented distances from each other around the outer circle of the auditorium, bleeding turquoise light over the proceedings.

Martin Norrell orated wonderfully, the sentiment of the humanist ceremony tugging at everyone's heartstrings.

Donny, unfortunately had hesitated, out of shyness, a little too long when he was told that he could now kiss his bride and much to the humour of all in attendance, Martha had grabbed her husband, nearly lifting him off his feet, and began sucking on his face. As their lips eventually parted, amidst whooping and clapping from the crowd, Martin reached behind himself and pulled the burning torch from its holder, handing it to the groom so that he could lead his wife to the bonfire. With everyone waiting for the festivities to begin, Donny touched the torch to the tiered pile of silver wood. The party had officially begun, but before the band had struck its first chord, a sonic boom tore the atmosphere to the north. All heads turned to see the gleaming silver teardrop corkscrewing towards them. Alexi and Serge's flyover was so fast and low that several guests dove to the ground. Commander Merchantim floated slightly higher over his monitor in the control room. His boys were home.

Deb Devaroux and Professor Steed danced in the crowd around the bonfire, a gold band melting in the heart of the conflagration.

The beginning of the end.